Elam

KATHI S. BARTON

World Castle Publishing, LLC
Pensacola, Florida
Copyright © Kathi S. Barton 2016
Paperback ISBN: 9781629893808
eBook ISBN: 9781629893815
First Edition World Castle Publishing, LLC March 21, 2016
http://www.worldcastlepublishing.com

Cover: Karen Fuller
Editor: Eric Johnston
Editor: Maxine Bringenberg

Prologue

"And you'll do this for us? For me?" The king wasn't so sure he wanted to trust her. Ariannona had been known to be somewhat flighty, and while she was a good person most of the time, he knew that she had bouts of behavior that got her into trouble. Anthony looked at Eve when she cleared her throat. She had to do this; life needed to be taken care of.

"What he's trying so hard not to do is tell you that we think you a bit off your head. But we know that it is only a front, is it not?" Eve smiled at him as she continued. "Anthony, she needs to know that we're not taken in by her ways. Try not to be so kingie and tell her we trust her."

Before he could voice his concerns, Ariannona spoke again, eyeing him like she knew what he was thinking. "You've asked me here for a favor. But you've yet to tell me how I will be able to do this. My lady, I know not of some of the things you're telling me." Anthony thought that she'd done it on purpose, adding the title to his lady wife. She wanted them to think that she'd forgotten that they were king and queen. "I'm but a person. No real magic, nothing to show for what I've been able to conjure. You know as well as I that though I am a witch of good standing, I'm not all that powerful. What you're asking me to do is well beyond my realm of knowledge, as I have said. Several times now."

"Come to me, Ariannona." Instead of doing what his lady wife commanded her to do, the witch took several steps back. "I wish to give you a gift, one that will help you with the task I have set before you." Her head was shaking hard now, as if she knew what was coming would change her forever.

And it would. Their hope and that of their children depended on this woman to do just what they told her. Asked of her. When she took another step back, Anthony had to fight hard with his frustrations. She had to do this.

"I have no wish of your magic, my lady. It is all that I can do to keep my own powers safely behind my teeth. And you know as well as I that I have been in trouble enough with it." Anthony nodded, knowing just how hard it was at times to keep your true self hidden. "And this thing you wish for me to do? I don't understand. You wish for me to visit your children, to give them a message, when there are no children of you. Or so we have been led to believe. And if there are said children, why are you not giving them the message on your own? There are many things that are not answered, and many more questions coming to me that I fear the answer to."

Anthony looked at his wife. Their children, six wonderful sons, had been born just that morning. They were hidden deep within the mountains to keep them safe. He and his lady wife knew that in a short time all that they were would be taken from them if things continued, including their lives. When Eve nodded at him, he got down off his chair and moved to stand with young

Ariannona. There were spies everywhere, he knew this. It was going to be their downfall.

"They are born. Six of them. They are hidden well but will be harmed, more than likely killed, should we announce their arrival." Ariannona nodded and he did as well. Tears, useless ones that he'd shed too often of late, filled his eyes and he continued. Emotions did not set well with a king, but a father could shed them freely. "Our lives will be taken, as will the castle, and without the help of a few magical beings as yourself, they will not have the tools that they'll need to care for each other. Much is at stake, Ariannona. More than we have time to explain to you now."

"And you think that I can take it to them. This message and favor you ask of me." Anthony nodded and kept an eye on his wife as she moved to stand behind the young witch. "You think...you said that your life will be taken with the castle. How is that possible when it is as magical as you? When the walls are forged of the greatest stones? Your men, they would die for you. Some even have."

"And they will, all of them. The castle will be great again one day, the magic restored with each new stone. But without your help, I'm afraid that all will be lost to all of us." Ariannona nodded and looked around the great hall. He wondered what she was thinking, what she might see that they had missed. "We need to give you a part of ourselves so that you can give them our message."

"And this part of you, it will give me what?" Anthony looked at his Eve, and she smiled sadly at him. "I don't think you're allowed to give me more magic. I have to earn that. And I am not able to do much because I'm not strong, like others. And to be honest with you, my king, I'm not so sure I'd like to be stronger than I am right now."

"You will have the gift of immortality. And of some magic that we can give you. Mostly knowledge. And as you get older, more will come to you naturally." Ariannona nodded and looked at Eve as she explained. "You must work hard while you wait for them. Stay out of trouble too. And when you do find them, I shall ask that you tell them how much we loved them."

"It will be long in coming, this message that you ask me to give to them. And a favor of some worth that you think I should take to them that you would trust me with it. That's why I need this gift; I will need the immortality in order to pass it to them." Anthony nodded when Eve did. "I think you jest with me. I don't think you tell me a falsehood, for I know you to be true. But this cannot be right. I think you have chosen the wrong person. Perhaps...perhaps you should ask Helena. She is a much stronger witch than I. Or Caroline. I know that both are used to magic and are very powerful."

"They have their tasks to do. And neither of you are to interfere with the other's set upon path. You may talk, converse, but never engage in any of their magic that might have to do with the castle or the people there." Anthony thought that was a good way to put things and admired his wife. But if only Ariannona could kill the witch, things would be so much the better even now. Well, that wasn't to be either. Things needed to progress. As they were set to do.

The door to the chamber they were in was banged upon. When Ariannona turned to look, he and his lovely bride of centuries past touched the younger woman at the same time. The ploy worked. She was distracted and they moved. Time was running short and they needed her to help them.

Her scream tore through him. He knew that it wasn't pain…well, perhaps a little of it was, but mostly it was the magic that filled her up that had her screaming. Magic that she would need to keep alive, and a message, the favor that they asked of her to give to his son. A son he'd never meet.

Pain entered his heart. So much was going to be lost to them. He wasn't a man who dwelled much on what he could not control, but this, this was something that would pain him until his last breath. His children would never know him. He'd never see them grow into men. Anthony would not even lay to rest near his own beloved.

As they laid Ariannona gently to the floor, her body quiet now that they were no longer filling her needs, they watched her carefully as her body took on a different look. He'd known it would happen, that she'd change, but he'd not known that it would do this to her. The magic would take as much as it gave to her.

Where her hair had been short, chopped no doubt by her own hand, it grew out long, well past her hips, he'd bet. And instead of the dark color that it had been, it was now white. Not a gray that it might have been with age, but as white as the snow that covered the ground even now. When she opened her eyes without moving, he could see the change in her eyes too. Gone were the brown they were before. They were the most startling color of silver that Anthony had ever seen. Magic danced in them even as she lay so still, almost in death. But he could see the snap of her anger even without her words.

"You did that a-purpose." He nodded. Still she hadn't moved, but they watched her. "I feel…I think to say I feel good, but it's so much more than that, isn't it?"

"You are of a good health and have much more magic, not in all things but a good deal more than you had before.

Or would have ever had should you have lived out your normal life." She asked him how long that might have been. "You would have been gone from this world today, as soon as you had stepped from the castle if you had told us no. It was the reason for the urgency."

Ariannona sat up slowly. He did not reach to help her, his own magic still there to share with her, but she seemed to understand and did not scold him when he did not. She was standing tall. He nodded to her when she ran her hands down her tattered clothing and it changed as she did. She would learn what she could do quickly now, her body humming of the power within her.

The clothing was gone, in its place a dress of white…as white as her hair had become. The only show of color on any of her was her lips, and they were as blood red as she was white. He laughed when Ariannona snapped her fingers and a single flower, a beautiful blue rose, appeared. After sniffing the fragrant flower, she put it on her shoulder, over her heart, and looked at them.

"You have given me a great deal, more than you wished, haven't you?" Eve, his queen and hers, nodded. "And this favor. What is it that you wish for me to tell your sons?"

Anthony nodded. It was done. And in a few thousand years, more than he could think on, this woman would be as important to his sons and their counterparts as she was to them at this moment. As Eve told her what she was to tell them, Anthony moved to his chair. His sons…as before, all he thought of was the loss.

He'd never see them grown, not even see them born. He and his wife, they would not see them darken the skies with their wings, not see them find their way in life. Not be there to guide them should they need it. Anthony would miss holding them in his arms, seeing them take their first steps, their first flight. They were going to miss it all if things, as they stood now, were not to change. He looked at Eve when she sat beside him. The woman, Ariannona the witch, was now gone.

"She will be a fine addition to them." He nodded, his heart too tender to speak of it. "Perhaps all of this perpetration, it is for naught. Perhaps the other will not bring us to ruin."

"You know as well as I that it is set in motion. That when the new storm blows, things will be out of our hands. People, our people, will rise against us. We will be no more. I know not when, but we do know that it will happen. I only wish that you could live, to be there with our children." She told him what she'd been saying for centuries, that she could not live without him. "I love you, my wife. With all that I am."

"And I love you, he who holds all that I am." She laid her head on his shoulder, and he held her. "My heart breaks for them all. I know that...while we have done all that we can to help them, I still think we have missed more than we can know."

"We will put others in place. People, dragons that will know what we have tried to do and the why of it." He felt her nod and wrapped his arm around her tighter. "I shall miss them, all the people here, the ones to come and the people we are begging for help."

"Jacob and Sally, they will be good to them. Care for them while we cannot. We have chosen well in them. You think?" He nodded. Just as she was to tell him more, things she had said to him over the last weeks, a storm blew into their windows and over their bodies. He was sure that Eve could smell the black magic as well as he could. "It has begun."

"It has."

There was no hope for it now. Things, as they had seen, were now coming. Their deaths, while not how they would die but that they would, had been shown to them. He held her while the storm, a great monster of a thing, blew around the castle walls and into their broken hearts.

Chapter 1

The ground was soft, but she was still exhausted, trying to plant the small seeds within the welcoming ground. Lindsey had been at this for hours, working the ground, and realized almost right away she might have bitten off more than she could chew. Putting her hand over her growing belly, she smiled down at the small plants that she'd put in the ground the day before.

They were already sprouting up, their tender leaves stretching to the sun. She knew it was beans, her favorite thing to eat, raw or cooked, and had put them in the ground first. Even the potatoes were coming up, the small curls of green just peeking through the dark of the earth.

"You'll wear the two of you out. Don't you want me to come help you?" Jacob was moving across the two yards toward her, a plate in one hand and a glass in the other. The man was forever pushing food at her and Essie. It was as if they weren't fat enough and he thought them to be bigger. She took the tea but left the sandwich alone. "Here, let me at least turn the earth for you. I swear you'll have that little man here if I don't watch over you."

He was spading the ground when she moved to the deck to sit. She and Essie were large with child, but unlike the other woman, Lindsey was having a good pregnancy while Essie had been sick nearly every day since just after Christmas. When she heard her talking to herself, or perhaps one of the little dragons that seemed to be everywhere these days, Lindsey watched her.

"I swear to you they think me an incompetent. I can do more with one hand tied behind my back than they can do all day." Lindsey asked her who when Essie sat down beside her. "Asher and Kiaran. I was as glad to see them leaving this morning as I was to be able to get up without puking ten times."

"You didn't get sick today?" Essie said she was slightly nauseous but not puking. "Well, that's wonderful. I was getting worried for you."

"Me too. But Caroline gave me some tea, and since I've been drinking it before bed, I've been feeling better every day. And the slightest smell doesn't send me to my knees in front of the commode." Jacob muttered something and they both laughed. Essie asked him what he'd said.

"I said I tried to tell you to call her a mite sooner. I was as worried as I could be about you and that babe of yours." He'd dug up the neat little row for her, and Lindsey got up to put the seeds in it. "I got it now, don't I? I'm doing this so that them boys of mine won't come here and scream at me for letting you get too tired again. Durn near had to sleep in the barn, they were so upset with me."

They'd not said a word and Lindsey knew it. Jacob was just a wonderful old man that loved them all very much, and wanted them to not think he was soft. Which everyone knew. When the sky above them darkened for a few seconds, they all looked up. The men were coming home.

Not Elam or Asher, however. They'd gone to the city to pick up a few things. Straw for one thing, the dragons so loved to roll in it. As well as some things that Elbert had needed for the house. Elam also had to close up his business, having sold it some time back for a good sum of money.

Daisy, her watcher and one of the smaller dragons on the property, came to her and sat on her knee. It was still something that she had to get used to, having dragons that were not her own around all the time, but they were for the most part a wonderful addition. Daisy had the task of keeping her straight…her head, anyway.

Ada, sister to one of the dragons who had died, was still hurting from the death of her brother Dawod and didn't come around much. But the rest of them, about ten of them now, came and went as they pleased, but never leaving the land or the magic that kept them safe. When Jed came to sit with them, he picked her up as if she didn't weigh nearly a ton, or so she felt, and put her on his lap. Zak landed in the yard softly, then shifted to his human self. Her mates were here and life was suddenly very good again.

"My lady." Lindsey looked at Daisy, who had been moved off her when Lindsey had been picked up. "My lady, there is someone coming. Someone that has been sent by the queen."

Lindsey looked over at Essie, who by all rights was the queen of them all, and was surprised when she shook her head. Lindsey looked around, just because Daisy made it sound as if this person was coming now. She'd come to realize that dragons, no matter the size, had a different time reference than she did. She supposed that it was because they'd been around for nearly forever. Right now could mean hours from now. Later might have been a month to them. And when they told you sometime, you might well have just not been told. It might be years or so before it even came to pass. Zak told her he'd keep the timeframe on track for her.

"They're beyond the trees. Not yet on our land." She looked at Jed when he spoke in her ear. "All I can tell you is not human, in the event that you didn't know. Whoever it is, they've been there for several days. Just watching us. I cannot tell what it is, but they are there. And magical."

"What does this person want? Do you know?" He said that he didn't. "Okay, so we just wait for them to come to us? Or are they planning to murder us in our beds? I have to tell you, Jed, I'm going to be very pissed if this person comes into our room and we're playing."

"As will I." As they all laughed, Lindsey reached out beyond to feel for the dragons. She was afraid for them, all of them coming here with a slayer out there trying to kill them. And even the few that were here already might be in danger still. There was a monster chasing them, a person that they knew nothing about, and even less as to his reasons for trying to kill one of these beautiful creatures. When Jed told her that it was time for supper, they entered the house ahead of her and she reached out again. This time she felt them, though very slightly.

You're out there, aren't you? Lindsey felt the stirring grow a little, of someone that was trying to hide from her. And for some reason she knew that it wasn't the man, the monster. *Are you friend or foe? Do you mean us harm?*

Nay, I do not. You are the keeper of the dragons, are you not? The one that calls them to you? Lindsey said that she was. *And you are not a dragon. How is that possible?*

I don't have a single clue. I do know that should you try to harm them, I will hunt you down in a minute. The person—because she wasn't sure if it was male or female as yet—stirred in her mind again. *You'll not breach it. I've been told I have a lock on my mind tighter than Fort Knox.*

I know of that place. I have been there, several times. It is easy to get in and out of if you know how. Lindsey told the person that she had no doubt if you were magical. *And you believe that I am? That I have some power over you?*

I never said you had more power, nor did I say that you had anything over me. But I am strong. Come out and I'll show you. The person politely declined. *Up to you. But you're coming here, to talk to us, right? The dragons know that you're there.*

I should like to give you some information. You may or may not already know. But there is a man here. He hunts what you keep close to your heart. The dragons. I have spoken to him. Today as a matter of fact. She asked if the person was known to them. *Only in that his heart is gray, not black, and that he is set upon his course no matter what the others have warned him about.*

Thank you for that. The person said it wasn't necessary. *But it is to me. Why do you hide from us? Why not come here where we are? If you fear for your life, we can protect you.*

I have no need of your protection. But I thank you for it. And I will wait for another time to visit. The one I seek isn't there. I have a message for him. Lindsey asked who it was. *I don't know the name, only the face. I was sent to give a message to him and him only.*

There are only two missing from here now. Can I assume that it's one of them that you need to talk to? Lindsey expected her to say something, that she was coming back, but nothing. *Who are you?*

A witch. Not necessarily of good standing, but I am to be trusted with this. It was a bargain that I made long ago. A promise that I will keep, should it be allowed. Lindsey wasn't surprised that she was more than likely old. And now that she knew her to be a witch, the gender of her voice changed to show her female. *I shall return in two days' time. Until I return to speak with him, I will keep an eye on the man who hunts. He has slayed two of your dragons. And one that died with you.*

Dawod. The woman said nothing. And when Jed came out on the porch, he didn't speak when she shook her head. *You are welcome here if you wish. There is shelter and plenty of food should you want that.*

I will return in two days. I will message you when I have information on your hunter. Lindsey thanked her again. *Your babe? You know that it is mostly dragon, some other magic that I cannot tell as well. Dragon young are a rarity nowadays. You are aware of what someone would do with such a child?*

Yes. I'm careful. No one will touch what is mine. If she thought the woman would answer her, she was disappointed. After moving to Jed's arms and telling him of the conversation, he simply held her. "I don't think she means us harm, but she does have a message for Asher."

"She told you his name?" Lindsey asked him who else it could be for. "I don't know. But I guess Asher would be my guess too. And she gave you no indication as to what the message might be? Maybe we can get him home sooner for her."

"No, just that she'd return in two days. I don't think it's necessary to have him rush home. I know he's busy." Lindsey looked out over the fields and knew that the woman, the witch, was there just on the edge, waiting. But for what, she didn't have a clue. "Jed, she's a witch. Do you think Caroline might know who it is?"

"I have no idea. But we'll ask her. She's coming back soon as well. And bringing you more seed. Though where you'd plant it is beyond me. We're going to have a garden big enough to supply armies now."

Maybe, she thought, but she was driven for some reason to have plenty to eat. It might have been her upbringing or something else. But food was going to be needed, and she was going to make sure that they had it.

~~~

Elam stretched his neck and felt it pop into place. He wanted to go home. Now, today, and not be bothered with this anymore. The man who had bought his business a few months ago had been putting him off for days now, and he was getting sick of it. The check was in the bank and had cleared nicely, so he wasn't sure what the put off was about. Elam was glad now that he'd had his banker cash out the money and not deposit it. There was something very fishy about this deal. Now the paperwork had yet to be signed making it a legal sale. And sitting here in the lawyer's office was making his dragon insane. The both of them were on edge.

Do you think him to change his mind? It would be like him, I think, to back out now when we have such plans. Casdon, his counterpart and the dragon to his man, chuckled. *To think that we are close to having the castle ready to start the repairs and rebuild, and now this happens and we have to wait here. I wish we could return and be working on it with the others. Don't you?*

Yes. Asher too. When we called home this morning, Jed said that they had the entire lower levels cleaned out and had found several things they couldn't wait to show us. The kitchen was located too, and now we're ready to begin laying the stones back as soon as the lower levels are put together by the magic we have.

The low growl from Casdon made him smile. The man across from him, Asher's lawyer, just grinned too. He told Jamie that in ten more minutes he was going to get up and leave.

It wasn't as if Elam needed the money, but he did need to have this finished. He didn't want to come to the city anymore. Not to stay. The family was at home, their family home, and he wanted to stay there as well. The castle, as they had talked about, was coming along nicely. The furniture was being built to the specs that they'd been given, and even some of the local women, a group of them from the local nursing home, were making rugs, rag rugs they'd been called even back in his father's time, to put on the cold stone floors when they were finished.

They'd been working on it for the better part of a year now. Moving the fallen stones had been the hardest work, heavy too. Then there had been minor and some major upsets along the way. A monster in the sublevels, a witch that tried to kill Asher, and a neighbor that had to be taken care of by one of the dragons to save their lives. Things, he supposed, were not normal, and he loved every minute of it, now that it was over and everyone was safe. And treasures had been found as well.

Hair combs were the most plentiful of women's things that were unearthed. Most of them in the lower levels were made of shells and wood. And they knew from reading books and talking to his dad that the lower levels, like the ones that held beds and other items, were used by the staff. Cleaning staff and the cooks from the kitchen above the ground had used it as their homes. Some of the guard had also been known to sleep in the lower levels, his dad said, when the weather was just too bad to go out.

Three swords had been found in the rubble. Two of them had the same marking, a dragon on the pummel, and the blade still, even after all this time, shone brightly in the daylight. They knew those to be of the castle guard. The other they assumed was from the men who had stormed the castle that night. The very swords that were part of the death of the king.

Several dozen plates had been found in the kitchen area, saved from the fall off the walls by the stone shelves that held them. The large ovens were in good condition, but they weren't sure if they were going to replace them with modern things or not. A table, long and made of wood long since gone from this area, had been found almost in perfect shape but for the legs. It had been pulled from the rubble and put with the other items they were going to repair or simply clean up.

Caroline had been able to gather them seedlings of trees that were long gone. They'd been planted by Essie, and were now sturdy trees that they were going to use when they made the items found of the same wood. There were other woods, too, that she'd brought to them…tall trees they'd become, to shade the castle in the summer and shelter it in the colder months. And with Essie's gifts — powers, he supposed they were now — they were growing saplings of their seedlings alongside the castle keep.

Anything made of cloth had been ruined long ago. They had bits and pieces of some of the tapestries that were still colorful, but full of holes. Someone had mentioned trying to find someone to repair them, and one of them had begun the task of looking for someone reliable. A few bits of a blanket and mattress were there as well, their use apparent when found on a bed that had long since been turned to rot.

Pottery vases—some broken, some in good condition—had been set aside. The pieces were going to be turned into something else rather than just wasted and thrown away. And no matter the shape they were in, they were put aside reverently and kept safe for use later.

Essie had suggested that they frame what cloth they found, and that they set up their own displays of things, like vases and carved stone, to show their children and their children too. Lindsey thought that they should mark where it had been found, along with what they thought it might have been used for. The women thought that the stone shelves along the wall to the main hall would do nicely for the things that they wanted to keep and treasure.

"He's here." Elam didn't bother standing when Jamie's secretary came in with a pitcher of water and made the announcement. This was not going to go well if the man didn't sign off on the paperwork. His attorney asked to speak to Elam's, and that was when he stood up.

"You signing today?" The man, Donald Proctor, looked at his attorney but didn't answer. "I asked you a question. Are you signing off on this today? I'm sick and tired of making this trip only to be told that you'd been hung up or that something came around. You're here; are you signing off on this now?"

"There are some...issues with Mr. Proctor and his family and business. Some unexpected problems. We wanted to see about cancelling the contract now and having the check returned, with a fee to you for your trouble. We will, of course, pay any legal fees you've incurred as well. I'm sure you understand. Things happen." Elam was shaking his head even before the man finished. "Sir, there isn't any way for him to complete this sale. Perhaps at a later day, but—"

"The sale is complete but for him getting his name on the paperwork. The money I have currently in my account says so." Proctor asked him when he'd deposited it, sounding upset. "I didn't deposit it, I cashed it out. I did it this morning after waiting the ten days that you asked me to do. I had the bank take the money right out of the account immediately so that I could have the cash in hand. I had a feeling this was going to be a problem. And if you read the fine print on the pre-agreement contact that you did sign, it says that you would pay me the rest of the money in thirty days. If not, then you are going to be in for a huge letdown. You now have...twenty-one days to come up with the rest of the money, or I own you."

"You bastard." Mr. Proctor lunged at him, and Elam waited for the hit. As soon as the fist, a soft one he noticed, hit his jaw, Elam let it take him to the floor.

No, he wasn't hurt, and the punch did nothing more than bloody his lower lip, but it was all he needed. He looked over at his attorney while still in a prone position. He smiled at her when she asked him what he wanted her to do now.

"Would you please file the paperwork needed to own Mr. Proctor?" Elam's attorney, Jamie Truman, smiled as she pulled out her cell and started making calls. Elam looked at the two men, Proctor and his attorney. "You have just made the biggest mistake of your life."

"Now see here. Tempers are high and there wasn't any reason for you to provoke me." Jamie laughed as she pulled the phone from her ear and looked at him with a grin. "You have her stop this right now. There isn't any reason for it. I've been under a great deal of stress of late."

"How much?" Instead of answering her he looked at Proctor. Elam stood up and Proctor backed from him. Jamie asked him again how much he wanted.

"You sign the paperwork now and pay me what you owe me and I won't take everything you own. Including the house on the lake that you bought for your mistress three months ago. Nor will I go to the papers about your three children that I'm pretty sure your new wife doesn't know about. I'm a man on edge too, and believe me, you do not want to see me have a bad day."

In the end Proctor signed the paperwork, and Jamie had a courier go to Proctor's bank and withdraw the balance of the sale in the form of a cashier's check and bring it to Elam. He said nothing as he gathered his coat and briefcase. It was done, and that was all he really cared about right now.

"You're a right prime prick, you know that, right?" Elam smiled and opened the door for Jamie when she was ready to go as well. Proctor said nothing more, and they made their way to the elevator.

"Remind me to never do business with you on a personal level. You are ruthless. You should be an attorney. I don't think you'd ever lose a case." He'd been one, he told Jamie, long ago. "Yeah, right. What are you, thirty? Less I'm betting."

"Much older than I look, I'm afraid." When she laughed again, he waited for the doors to open before he continued. "Thank you for today. If you ever need anything from me, just let me know. I'm done with corporate bullshit."

Handing her an envelope, he made his way to the front doors. He was ready to go home. And he really hoped that his brother was too. But before he could make good on his escape, Jamie stopped him before he was able to hail a cab.

"You can't do this." He said that he could and he did. "But my fee is...well hell, Elam, my fee is about one percent of this. This is all the money that Proctor just paid you. And the check is made out to...how the fuck did you do this? And why would you? Why would you have the bank make me the one to get this money?"

"You want to start your own firm, right?" She nodded but told him that wasn't in the cards for her. "It is now. You cannot only afford a sitter for your daughter while you work, but you can pay off the student loans you have, buy a reliable car, and get yourself started on the dream I know you've had for a long time. You did right by me, and I want to do the same for you."

"But this is over three million dollars. That's a lot of 'right' if you ask me." The cab pulled up in front of him and she stopped him again before he could get it in and make his escape. "I'll never forget this, Elam. Never. You've given me...you've given my family a great gift in this."

"Don't become jaded. And please, continue to be the person and the lawyer that you are. One who tries her cases with her heart, not her wallet." She nodded and he kissed her on the forehead. "Now. If you need me, you know how to get in touch with me. I want you to have a great life."

"I will. Now. Thank you again. I'm not sure that I'll ever be able to repay you for this." He said that he didn't want her to and slipped into the cab. "Elam, would you really have taken him for everything he had? Proctor, would you have had me go through with what you wanted me to do had he not signed the paperwork?"

"And then some."

The cab slid into traffic and he leaned back on the seat. Casdon told him he was a sap and Elam told him to fuck off.

Asher was finished up as well. So instead of waiting until the next morning to drive back home, the two of them decided that they'd go now, pick up the things they needed on the way, and sleep in their own beds tonight.

"I talked to Essie earlier. She said a woman wants to talk to me." Elam asked Asher about what. "Don't know. She's not human, a witch Lindsey said, but that's about all they know. Apparently she can communicate with Lindsey without any contact. Essie thinks she might be working for us in a way to keep the dragons safe from some hunter that's been out there. I think she might know who he is."

"You think she's in trouble, this witch?" Asher shrugged and told him he guessed he'd find out. "I don't envy you having a mate and all this responsibility. I like my life just the way it is. Now that this business is done, I'm ready to get on to more important matters. Like where to put my big screen television in my new home."

Elam hadn't been sure that he wanted his own home. But he knew that things were getting tight in the house. Not that he'd been asked to move out...on the contrary, they'd told him it was his home too. And it wasn't as if he had moved far away. He was less than a hundred yards from the main house and his brother's new home. But with the new babies coming—both Lindsey and Essie were breeding—he and Casdon wanted some space to call their own. He supposed it was time to leave the nest, as it were.

We're going to be single for a very long time, you and I. He had been single for a long time, he told Casdon. *Yes, we both have, but the thing is, now we can have chickens over whenever we want.*

Chicks, and I don't think Dad will approve of us having our own little dragon fuck fest. No matter how old we are. He is still Dad. Casdon told him he didn't have to know. *Right. Dad knows everything.*

His dad gave the best hugs, and Elam found that he needed one of those as well right now. He really hated the city and all the things that went with it. He didn't mind the town, the one that was pretty close to where they lived, but the city and all the noise and smells? Elam was a man who liked his peace and quiet.

Chapter 2

Ariannona sat on the earth and watched the birds at play. It was quiet here, if one could discount the four billion bugs making noises, the birds' endless chatter, and every living thing going about their business. Smiling, she thought about the pair of lion cubs she'd seen yesterday and her conversation with them. They'd told her about the house, and the men and women who worked on it. Also the bodies that were being pulled from the mother earth.

They've been digging there for three months now, and it seems there is no end to it all. Ariannona said that she'd seen it. *I will be glad for it when they're done. The lake fingers run by that land, and the water there is the cleanest in all of the valley. And the sweetest too.*

There had been police and other personnel at one end of the king's property. She knew that the man there had murdered and that he'd buried the dead on his land. He'd also used the caves, something that had bothered her a great deal more than him killing anyone. The caves had been her home for the better part of the last two thousand or so years. Whoever had found out and set things to right, she was happy for it. The lion asked her if she had any more information on the goings on.

"They'll be gone soon. The land has nothing more to give them."

The last body would be found soon. They were close now and she'd used a little of her magic to guide them closer to it. It wasn't cheating, as she had been told she could not do, nor could she interfere with the way things were set in motion. But since they were close to the last body, it didn't count as her making them do something that they weren't already doing anyway. Ariannona had learned that she really couldn't cheat the hard way.

Ariannona had just left the castle after seeing the king and queen when she'd come upon Helena the black. At that moment she knew that the queen had been right...her death would have happened then had she not been warned to tread carefully. The witch had never cared for her, and Ariannona had disliked her as well. But this time she saw Helena trying to whip up some of the men in the village into a fight and had moved in to calm things. The fight, as it turned out, had netted her a stay in shackles, and the three men were dead anyway.

The worst part about being in the shackles, a way to subdue women like her, a witch, was that she had to endure having no time out of doors. Where anyone could come by and beat her for no other reason than she was there and unable to get up to fight back, as well as throw their rubbish on her. Fourteen days after she was released, a short sentence by most standards then, she went to find the people who had hurt her. Ariannona mourned the death of her king and queen, but others, mostly the ones that were easily manipulated, were ready to do more harm and damage to anyone that would cross their paths.

Not only could she not find them, but she was pretty sure that they'd ended up on the bad end of some powerful magic. Namely Helena the black. She found out later that they'd been used for her coven, and Ariannona had left the area for a few years.

A breaking sound behind her had her pulling the darkness that was forever part of the woods, no matter the time of day, around her.

"I know that you're here." Ariannona said nothing as the person moved nearer to where she was lying. "I have a question for you. You said you knew what I was about. I want you to tell me if I really did kill that dragon."

"Why?" Her voice was all around him. She'd pitched it so that the man would have no idea where it had come from. "You think to make a profit off his death? I assure you that you have not read your lore about them well if you think you can pick over his carcass."

"He's dead then." The man did a little dance and asked her again where he was. "I killed him. It's only right that his body become mine. And I know my lore, as you call it, better than anyone. I have all the rights to whatever magic I can get."

"His is no more." He asked her what that meant. "Simply that. There is no body for you to sell off in bits and pieces. There is no rich dragon blood for you to drink. And the magic that he had, since he did not die close to you, went to someone else. I would imagine the female with him at the time."

"Well that's not fair." Ariannona laughed. "Stop laughing at me. I know my rights from the death of a dragon. I have given him the killing blow, and by the rights and laws of his kind, he is mine to do with as I please."

"You really are quite stupid, aren't you?" He sputtered again. "How did you know that I was here? You are a mere human. You have no magic. What did you do to find me?"

She watched him carefully, and when he glanced up into the tree beyond him, she looked too. It was hard to find at first, but once she did, she was pissed about it. He'd set up cameras to find her. And dragons, she thought. Now she understood why he'd been able to track the large beasts.

"I'm stealthy." She would imagine that he might think he was. But he was a blundering fool as he moved through the woods. "Where are you? I don't like not being able to see you. Come out of hiding and let's talk, you and I. I'm lonely for someone to talk to."

"That is really too bad on your part. I've no wish to have any sort of conversation with you. I think you a fool and believe that you should leave soon, before you are killed." Using her magic, a power that was given to her by the king and queen that fateful day, she found nine cameras around the general area where she was, as well as a dozen or so back at his campsite, ready to be hung.

Blowing them up sounded like a great idea, but she paused. He'd only replace them. Instead, she figured out how they worked and looped the serene quietness of the woods so that to him, it would look like nothing was ever in his camera's eye. Before she pulled back from her work, she remembered that they would be running all the time and added a little dark time to the loop.

"Mistress?" Ariannona looked at Izic when he landed in front of her. "He has returned to the magical place."

The brownie, the smallest of the magical creatures that had been around as long as dragons, had been with her for so long. Someday she would have to remember hard when he'd come to be with her. Izic had no one but her, and she the same with him. They helped each other. She kept him alive with her magic and he informed her when she needed information about something. Plus, he was her only friend and the only person, human or otherwise, she trusted without question.

"I have to get this human out of the way so that I can move." He nodded and grinned at her. "You know that we cannot harm him. His path is set, whatever that might be."

"He is a dragon slayer. A monster to my kind and others." She told Izic that she was sorry about that, but he knew the rules. "I know them as well as you, mistress, but it does not mean that I like them."

"Me either. Most of the time." He nodded and told her that he would help her. "Just don't hurt him. You can...what are you going to do?"

"He is very tired." Ariannona smiled. It was a great plan, but she cautioned Izic that the sleep was not to be permanent. "Nay, mistress, only for a few moments, time for you to escape from the ground."

As soon as the man simply dropped to the ground she looked at Izic, who said he was sorry. "You most certainly are not. I'm not mad, but what would we have done had you harmed him when he fell? Perhaps he might have hit his head too hard and not been the same. Not that he doesn't deserve it. But we cannot interfere. The king made that perfectly clear."

"We have only given him a short rest, so that he might be better equipped at whatever course he is set out to do." She wasn't sure that wasn't the same thing as interfering, but stood up and moved out of the area. Ariannona told

Izic about the cameras as she made her way to the magical property.

"You have learned a great deal, mistress, by working with your computer." She told him it was easy once you figured out a few things. "I have no such thing to help me. I'm much too small to even carry such an item. And I would be worn to nothing, hopping from one key to the next to say anything on the screen."

She stopped walking and turned to look at him. When he winked at her, she laughed. The things he said to make her feel better about her day. As they continued on their way, she asked him about the man, the slayer.

"He has a small home, though larger than even yours when you are here. And it can be conveyed from one point to another by simply starting it up with that smelling machine in the front of it. He can make it bigger or smaller too, by simply pushing a button and waiting." She told him what it was. "Camper. You should perhaps find you one of those. It would be nicer than sleeping upon the ground. I myself would find it most nice when it is raining or very chilly."

"You wouldn't like it any better than I would. First of all, it's all closed up. There are windows on them, but it's not nearly as lovely as the fresh outdoors. And there is no view. Who would want to sleep where you couldn't see the stars at night or the feel the sun coming up over the mountain?" He said that he would surely miss that part. "Me too. And we have the sense to get in out of the rain, do we not? I think we'd not like where we had it parked and be moving it around all the time."

"Yes, we do have a great deal of freedom that I don't believe he has." He flew to her shoulder and landed there, holding onto her hair as she moved. "He has books and drawings. None of them look like any of the dragons that are on the king's land. Recently he has more equipment in the small hut...camper. I have seen such things when you go into town, but his are shinier. I think he tracks the dragons by their cold."

"Cold?" He said that was what he noticed. The temperatures of the settings were very low. "He thinks that dragons are cold then. That's the dumbest thing...does he not realize that they have the breath of the hottest places of the land? That they can boil him alive with only a small breath?"

"He is most stupid." Ariannona didn't think that was right either. The man had killed poor Dawod. "I have other creatures watching out for him as well. Bear, he is most happy with his assignment to chase the slayer when he gets close to the castle ruins."

Bear was her friend as well. She'd saved him once from another hunter when he came upon the big bear while he'd been fishing. Every day for a month after that, Bear would bring her fish. She finally told him she was but one person, and a dozen or so fish daily was too much. Now he only brought her one when she asked. It had worked out well for them both.

The big house came into view and Ariannona noticed that a third and fourth house had been added surrounding the property. She wondered which son, if it was one of them, had the magic that could do such a thing, and realized that it mattered little. She had a favor to complete for the king and queen, and then she was finished.

"I shall miss you, Izic." He told her that he would make sure that her body was properly cared for. "Thank you. I must say, I'm looking forward to getting this finished in a great way, but will be saddened that I will leave this earth. I have so enjoyed it for the most part. But the queen, she promised me that I would see her again, and that will be lovely. She was a good woman."

"And the king a good man." Ariannona nodded. "You are not sure yet, are you, if I will join you?"

"Nay, I don't think so. She said that I would be rewarded when I completed this task, and that I would someday see the king and queen for my efforts." It had been worded strangely, she would admit that. "I have set you free, you know...you are welcome to go and have many children of your own."

"I should like that, I think. Perhaps I will name one for you." Izic flew off then, something startling him, she knew. Before she could turn to find out what was coming upon them, she felt the claw at her throat and the dragon's breath on her cheek.

~~~

Casdon had been moving over the tree tops for over an hour when he spotted the woman. She wasn't hard to spot really, dressed as she was, her hair as white as the snow on the mountain tops this time of year. When he saw her so close to the edge of their land, he knew that he had to keep her away. There had been too much shit going on of late for him to take any kind of chance. Casdon licked a path along her neck to her shoulder, and nearly let her go when she moaned.

What are you doing here? He knew that she could understand him. Casdon could taste her magic and knew her to be very powerful. *I asked you a question, and I know you can answer me this way.*

"I came with a message." He didn't let her go, but felt drawn to bring her body closer to his. As his dragon, he knew that he had to be careful not to harm her, but the need to feel her pressed closer to him made him shift. "You're one of the dragon hatchlings."

"I am. And you are?" She didn't answer him. Running his hand down her body, telling himself he was looking for weapons, he felt her full breast in his hand, her nipple hardening in his palm. He nipped gently at her throat and was rewarded with another moan. "I want to taste your flesh."

Turning her around, he lifted her body up and took her mouth. It was warm, sweet, and her tongue danced along his as he deepened the kiss. Moving to a tree, he pressed her body to it as he lifted her dress, and feeling her warm muscled thigh in his hand nearly made him whimper.

"Hurry." He wasn't sure he'd heard her say that or if he'd only been telling himself to hurry when she pulled at his shirt. As her mouth moved down his chest to his own nipple, he pulled at her blousy top until it was nothing more than shreds. As soon as she bit down on his hard nipple, he tore the rest of her clothing off.

"I need you." She nodded, pulling at the top of his pants. Lifting her breast up to his mouth, he feasted on her, suckling at her as hard as he could until she jerked his head up from her. "I need you."

"Take me." He nodded, lifting her up so that her pussy was nearly wrapped around his cock. He rocked into her, watching her face as she held onto his shoulders. "Please. I need to feel you inside of me now. I know not why, but to feel you there will complete me."

His body stiffened as he held her. Complete her. His making love to this woman would complete them both, and that scared him. Dropping her down from his body, Casdon took two steps back and then two more when she reached for him.

"You're my mate." She shook her head, and he nodded. "You are. You're the one that would...do you think you are to complete us both?"

"Both?" The woman stood there, her hands moving to cover her nakedness, and then she was dressed. The white of her dress did nothing to hide what he now knew was beneath it. "You aren't my mate, you...you were just there and we had a need."

"You said I would complete you." She told him it had been a mistake. "Yes. That's it. A mistake. We were just...needy, and it occurred to us at the same time." She cocked a brow at him, and Casdon was reminded of Elam; he did that as well.

"You think so? That at the same time we both were so overcome with need that we sort of came to each other? I do not." The little brownie landed on the woman's shoulder and glared at him. "Go away." But before he could say anything, like he was, the brownie spoke to him.

"You should take what is yours, young dragon. You know as well as her that you are not needy. She is your mate." Casdon shook his head. "Mates come but once in a lifetime. Pushing her away is not the right thing to do."

"Hush, Izic. He's not my mate. You know what I must do today." Izic looked at her then back at him before the woman spoke again. "I am here to talk to one of the men that reside here. I have a message for him."

"Who?" She only lifted her chin for an answer, and he had the most incredible urge to kiss her again. "I'm not going to allow you to go onto the land without answers. Who is it you're here to talk to?"

"You think to stop me?" Casdon nodded at her. "I have been sent here by the king. He and his lady wife, they gave me a task to complete, and you will not keep me from it."

"Asher sent you here to talk to one of us?" She asked him who that was. "Never mind. All right, I'll allow you passage if you can cross over the magic."

He was sure that she'd not be able to. Casdon had a feeling that she was lying, and that nearly giving herself to him had been a trick to make him forget himself. There wasn't any way she was his mate. No way in hell.

But the moment that she stepped onto their land, Casdon began to have doubts about everything. Not about her being his mate...he was sure that had been something else. And the little brownie with her, he hung to her shoulder as if he might fall at any moment. Then he realized that she was stomping, and Casdon was glad that he was behind her so he could smile. He had a feeling if she could see him right now, he'd be a dead dragon.

What are you doing? The voice of Elam startled him into nearly missing a step. Casdon hadn't really been paying attention to his footing anyway. He'd been watching the way her bottom moved under her dress, knowing that her legs were long and strong, her bottom filled his— *Casdon? What the hell are you doing with that woman?*

Nothing. We didn't do anything. He realized how guilty he sounded and mentally shook himself. *She has a message for one of us. She won't tell me who it is so I can't tell you if you ask.*

About what? Casdon said he had no idea about that either, but that she claimed Asher sent her. *Asher is here with me. And he knows of no such message from a woman.*

By now they were at the main house. All of them, including his father and grandfather, were there as well. Even Lindsey and Essie, large with their babes, were seated on the porch watching and waiting for them. He looked to the sky when it darkened slightly just before his brothers landed to join the fray.

He didn't care for the way that Essie was grinning at him. He just knew that she'd been spying on him, and he wanted to deny whatever was in her head. But he kept glancing at the woman, and knew that even the most unobservant person could see his erection.

"Hello." Lindsey leaned back on her hands and stared up at them. "I spoke with you a few days ago, I think. I didn't catch your name."

"No, you didn't. I have a message for a son by the name of Casdon." Casdon looked at the men and women in front of him, knowing this was a joke. When the woman continued, Casdon turned and looked at Elam. "I spoke with his parents only days before they were murdered and they asked me, sort of coerced me, into coming here and giving you a message from them, but..."

"You're saying that you spoke to my parents and that they bullied you into coming here, some three thousand years later, to give me a message?" The woman turned and looked at him. "I don't believe you. Who are you and what are you trying to pull? Is this about not having sex with you in the woods? You're bitter because I don't want to have you as my mate?"

He knew that he'd made a mistake the moment that someone behind him laughed. But when Elam came to stand behind the woman, standing in front of him, he could see his anger and thought for sure it was because he'd nearly made love to this woman without telling him.

"Your father told me to come here. He said I was to tell you something after I gave you his gift. A gift that I was to hand you when I saw you." He took a step toward her and he could feel her magic as it grew. "He said...they both claimed that the people who raised you, Jacob and Sally Benson, would have raised you to be a good son, a better man. But I can see that they were wrong."

"Now you see here a minute. You can't be coming here and saying those things about my sons. None of them."

Jacob stood up and made his way down the stairs just as a sound echoed in the distance. Without thought to what he might be doing, Casdon jerked the woman around behind him and shoved at Jacob to get him down out of the line of the shot. Casdon took the bullet that not only tore through him, but hit the wood of the porch. He felt the moment the iron entered his body. Someone had just killed him.

As he fell to the ground he heard shouts. His body felt heavy, his head was spinning. Looking at his shoulder, he tried to tell himself that he'd be fine, but he could feel the poison as it raced through his body at an alarming rate. Opening his eyes that he'd not even realized he'd closed, he looked into the face of the most beautiful woman he'd ever seen. She was shouting at him to stay with her.

"You hurt?" She shook her head and he felt the air in his lungs simply rush out. "Good. Very good. I think...I'm pretty sure I'm going to die."

"Nay, you are not. Had you been here when I was told to come, then I would have given you this sooner." He felt weakened by the blow to his system, his own blood turning against him as it filled every part of him with the poison of the iron in the bullet. His heart sounded slow, his blood flow sluggish. "Casdon, look at me."

"I cannot." The pain to his face made him look at her again. "Did you hit me? I'm hurt and you hit me?"

"Do you wish to receive the gift of your sire and his mate?" He had a hard time focusing on her. "Casdon, listen to me. You must answer. Do you wish to receive the gift of your sire and his mate?"

His *yes* to her question brought to him the most incredible pain. His head felt as if a bomb had gone off. His body felt powered through by a large machine. And when he bowed up with the feeling of being stung by thousands of bees, he let his body slip over the edge, hoping that he'd simply just die now without lingering in this much pain forever.

Chapter 3

Ariannona wasn't sure what she was to do. Izic had just delivered some news to her that she was still trying to understand. When Essie had asked her to sit with young Casdon while she went to lie down, the brownie had come to tell her what he'd been able to find out about the slayer. But before she could tell Essie, she'd begged off for some rest.

For some reason, and she'd not mentioned it to the new queen, she thought the woman in good shape and in no more need of a nap than she was. When the door opened, Elam, Casdon's other half, came into the room and Ariannona started to leave.

"Please don't go. I'd like...if you don't mind, I'd like to have a conversation with you." She told him she knew no more than what she'd told the new king. "Asher. He said if you call him the new king again, he might go insane. Call him Asher."

"I cannot." Elam only smiled at her, but she did sit down again. "He will be well now. I'm sorry that he was injured. I had come to give him the magic from his parents' days ago, but he wasn't here. By the way, I think you all have the same magic as him. I can feel it on all of you."

"Thank you for that. And it's not your fault that he was shot any more than it is mine. But, he did what he did to protect you. Whoever it was shooting here, he was aiming at you. And I'd like to know why you think someone wanted you dead." Ariannona wanted to know as well, and had Izic out looking for the slayer to see what he'd done. She told Elam that she was looking into it. "You said that you had a message for Casdon. Can you tell me what it was?"

"Nay. It is his message." Elam nodded and looked at Casdon. "The gift that I gave him, it came with conditions. He will need to abide by them."

"I can't answer for him, but the rest of us, we'll make sure that he does it. Was he to pay you, give you some sort of boon for it?" Ariannona said no, just two rules. "All right. What happens to us now?"

"Us? I don't understand. If you mean that he thinks me his mate, then I know that to be impossible. I am to die once he has been given the message." He asked her why she thought this. "The king. He explained to me that I would see the king and queen then. Once he is given his gift, then I could see them."

Elam sat there for several minutes before he laughed. When she asked him what was going on, he only laughed harder. It wasn't until he stood up that she felt perhaps it had been a mistake to have sat with him. He was insane, she thought.

"Did they say that you would see them, Anthony and Eve? Or that you'd see the king and queen?" She didn't understand his question and told him so. "Humor me. What was it precisely? What did they say?"

"The queen said that I would be rewarded when I completed this task, and that I would someday see the king and queen for my efforts." She looked around the beautiful room and then back at the man on the bed. Everything they had said to her, the way that she'd been confused by the wording of the statement, now seemed to come clear. "She said that I would gain a great reward when I gave him the gift from his parents. That men would bow before me, worship me in ways that none had before or would after."

"I think she knew that you were our mate." Ariannona shook her head as Elam stood still. "You're our mate. Or at least you're Casdon's. I have no idea if you're both of ours, but it would stand to reason since the other women have become as such to our counterparts."

"I want no mates. I was to get...I thought I was to be given death. After all these years, I have prepared for it. Looked forward to it." He said nothing as she moved to the window of the room and looked out. "I've no use for a mate. I have no desire to have someone that I cannot rule in my life."

"Well, that at least we have in common." She looked at Casdon when he sat up on the bed. He was weak and still slightly pale, but she could see that he was gaining strength and that he would be well soon enough. "Have you touched her, Elam? To see if she belongs to you as well?"

"No. I don't think I want to know." It was both painfully honest and felt good to her that he no more wanted her than she did either of them. "I don't suppose you can just leave us alone and we get on with our lives as we had been before?"

"I have a message." Casdon asked her what it was. When the implications of what the message might mean hit her now, she shook her head. "It's a trick. It's always been a trick."

"More than likely." When Casdon stood up and moved toward her, speaking things that made her heart ache and her body burn, she backed up. "They knew that you'd bring me the message and that I would more than likely get hurt. They also knew, somehow, that you're our mate and that bringing you here would bring us together. Tell me the message and your name. I wish to say it."

"I don't...they said the love of Sally would bring forth the love of a mother." He nodded and touched his fingers to her throat. When she took another step back, to keep him from touching her more, she felt hands, strong and callused, touch her body from behind, and she knew it was Elam. "You said that you did not wish for a mate. If you touch me now, with the intent of what is in your mind and heart, we will not be able to go our separate ways."

Fingers touched her breasts, and her dress was lifted when Casdon went to his knees before her. His hands pulled at her body, massaging her in a way that made her tense, not relaxed. When she was naked, her dress and underclothing just gone, she felt Elam milk her breasts in his hands as her legs were parted.

"He's going to eat you. Then I will." She shook her head, but Elam only laughed in her ear. "I can smell you. The heat of your pussy. The way your body is ready for his mouth."

"I do not...no, you cannot." Ariannona looked down at Casdon when he touched her intimately. His body was nude, his hands at her hips. She could see his cock, ready and hard between his thighs, and wanted to feel it. Touch him. But the cock at her backside had her rocking into him as Elam continued to make love to her his way, with his hands and fingers.

The first swipe of Casdon's tongue at her pussy had her crying out. No man had ever touched her this way. Men had tried to take more than she was willing to give, but this, she had a feeling that this was going to be overwhelming and fulfilling at the same time. When she felt Elam turn her slightly, she thought him to be pulling her away from Casdon and sobbed in the back of her throat. But he took her nipple in his mouth and suckled hard on just the tip, enough that she had to hang onto him or fall.

The mouth at her pussy was indeed eating her. Each time Casdon brought her, taking her over the edge only to bring her back there to do it again. Elam was touching her breast, her neck, and even her navel as he made his way over her. Each touch of their fingers, each bite of their teeth on her flesh, was bringing her closer and closer to something that she knew in her heart was going to be the end of all that she knew.

"Please, you must let me breathe. I'm going to fall." The small laugh from one of them had her grabbing hair. When she looked into the eyes of Elam, his face hard with a need that she felt herself, her knees grew weaker, and she knew that she was going to indeed fall.

"Casdon, to the bed."

Yes, she thought bed. That's where she needed to be to think, to cover up from their hands. But as soon as she was prone, her body seemingly stretched out for them, she knew that whatever they'd done to her standing, they had doubled their efforts to...she wasn't sure what, but she thought them to claim her. It was all she could think of.

Elam slid down her body, Casdon now at her breasts. They were different in their making her body come alive. Casdon was hungry, his mouth and hands digging into her with a profound hope of devouring her. Elam, at her pussy, explored her, discovered new ways to bring her over, his fingers inside of her touching off newly explored sensations. When Casdon sat on her chest, his cock at her breasts, she cried out when he squeezed them together and fucked them hard. As she came, her body bowing up off the bed yet again, she felt a thick hardness at her entrance that scared her.

"Don't, love." She tried to calm, Elam's words like a balm to her frightened body. "I wish to enter you."

Casdon leaned over her, his cock now at her mouth, and she opened for him, just as the cock at her pussy slid deeper. It wasn't painful, but it was thick and something that was new to her. As soon as she felt Casdon enter her mouth completely, the cock at her pussy slammed forward and she screamed.

Neither of them moved. She could feel the tension in the room and realized that they were waiting on her. Ariannona looked up at Casdon and saw the pain on his face, and listened to his softly spoken words.

"Please, love. Don't bite down more."

She felt her mouth relax as the pain in her jaws begin to let up. As he sat there, his cock in her mouth and his hands gripping the headboard, all she could think about was that he was the most beautiful sight she'd ever seen. Then Elam moved, his cock stretching her more as he moved deeper, then back out slowly, gently, his body taking hers to new levels.

Casdon fucked her mouth, Elam her pussy. She was hard with the need to come. Her body was so close that she was afraid that when she released, she'd hurt them again. But when Elam touched his finger to her clit, pinched her, she screamed around the cock in her mouth that she was coming again, then a third time before she felt the first splash of Casdon's cock filling her mouth.

~~~

He wanted to taste her but knew that she'd be sore. Elam watched her as she slept, her body now curled around his and Casdon at her back. He had no idea why they'd taken her. They'd only just discussed how they didn't want a female in their lives, and now they'd not just taken one but taken her to their bed as well. He looked as Casdon when he whispered his name.

"She's beautiful." Elam nodded, his body rocking into hers even though he'd tried his best to tell himself she needed rest. "I want her again, to feel her wrapped around me."

"She's never had sex before us. We'll have to take it easy on her." Casdon nodded but his body, like Elam's, was having a difficult time waiting when she was naked between them. Reaching down to his cock, Elam stroked it trying to ease, even only for a bit, some of his overwhelming need to bury his cock deep inside of her again.

When her hand joined his, wrapping around his cock, he moaned and felt himself slide to his back when she moved his hand. Looking at her face, he saw that she was staring into his eyes even as she came up on one elbow. When her leg lifted, he knew that Casdon was entering her even as she leaned over and took Elam into her mouth. Christ, he nearly came when she swallowed his cock past her tight throat.

The bed moved in motion to the love making that Casdon was doing to her. Up and down her head bobbed on him, her hands at his balls, her breasts pressed tightly against his leg. When she shifted again, this time to be between his legs, he nearly came when Casdon lifted her ass up to his cock and took her from behind.

Now they were fucking each other. Her mouth was doing wondrous things to his cock. Her breasts swayed back and forth to the motion of Casdon's strokes. And when he held her head to his cock, Elam knew that when she came, she was going to bring him with her. As soon as Casdon cried out, he felt his own cock empty deeply into her throat as she fucked the last of his cum into her, the hum of her own release nearly taking his head off when he came again.

When she moved over his body, sliding up so that her head was now on his chest, Casdon moved to lay beside them and closed his eyes. Elam held her to him, hearing her heart beating slower and slower until, like his, it was at a normal pace again. However, he was under no illusions that anything was going to be normal again.

"My name is Ariannona." He looked at her when she sat up, her chin on her fist. "I thought perhaps it would serve no purpose to keep it from you now."

"No, not really. Not since I have tasted every part of you." Her face reddened and he told her he was sorry. "I never meant...we never meant to hurt you that way."

"I know that. But this does not lessen the fact that we are bonded and truly mates now. I never wanted it, and am still not sure that this was a good idea." He didn't want to lie to her and told her that he thought not as well. "But here we are. The three of us."

"You will stay then?" He knew that he sounded somewhat desperate, and he supposed in a way that he was. She was his now, his and Casdon's, and he didn't want to be without her now that he'd been with her. She looked over at Casdon, who snored softly. "He and I will care for you. Make sure that you have everything that you need. Anything that you might ever want too. We're family now, the three of us."

"I have what I need. I can care for myself." He didn't say anything because really, he knew that she was right. "The king and queen, Casdon's parents, they tricked me — and you — into this. Are you not angry with them? I am. Very much so. They might have been a little clearer in their statements. Instead of letting me believe that I'd die once I came to see him."

"No, I'm not mad at them, but I can see how you would be." And he really wasn't. "I might have been had you appeared in my life before today, or even before this decade, when there were no wives to my brothers. Then we were not where we are now in our lives. It's not to say that I'm not afraid…I am. Nor am I sure what sort of reasoning that they had for this. But I'm sure, like the other things that we've been told and have found out, that there was a good reason for this, and I'm sure that it will work out."

She laid her head on his chest again and Elam wrapped his arms around her. "I'm not so sure that it will. I'm set in my ways. I have things I like to do, most of which do not involve sharing my life with another person."

"Casdon and I can give you space. I'm not sure how much we can, because like you, we've been alone — well, mostly alone — for a long time as well. With only our brothers to keep us company." He looked around the room. "We had this house built because while we love our families, we like our quiet as well. There is a lot of noise when you have that many under one roof, and even being out of doors all the time like we are, it's still nice to have a place to call our own."

"I have a brownie. He keeps me company." He knew of the brownie, had talked to him actually. There were to date several dozen of them living on this property, and more coming in all the time. They served the dragons in ways that they could not. "He and I, we thought me to die when I came here. I'm having a hard time getting the thought out of my head that I will die now."

"To see the king and queen again, they told you. I think perhaps you will someday as well, but I think that's sort of funny." She said nothing but lifted her head again. "You were there when they died. I'm guessing you assumed that when you died, after this I mean, that you'd be with them? In the afterlife?"

"Yes." She shifted on the bed and he felt her pain at it, and knew that they'd been too rough with her. He was about to suggest a bath or a long hot shower when she continued. "I thought the guard was joking when he summoned me to the castle that day. I was...still am...nothing compared to the other witches of that time. There was Helena the black, of course, and Caroline the white. They were not...either of them would have been better at the job than me, and I think I knew that even then. I even suggested to them that they should call for their help."

"Helena is dead." She nodded, and he guessed that she'd know that. "Caroline, she comes here sometimes to help us with issues. Even Gobi, do you know her? She owns a shop in town that we call to for answers as well."

"Gobi, she is a new witch. Neither good nor bad because she's made no such decisions on what she wants to be. I am gray, I guess you could say, neither white nor black. Just because of the clothing I wear people think me white, but I make choices to be good over evil when I see things. I saw what evil magic does to a witch when she is on the wrong path, so I have not gone fully to that point. And I have no title either, as does Caroline. I simply practice the white arts of magic, not the black. But Helena is not the only evil person in the world. Once one of them tried to murder me when I meant no one any harm." Casdon, who was awake now, asked her what had happened. Instead of answering him, she stood up and turned her back to them.

The long jagged scar that ran from her shoulder to her thigh was white with age, thin now that her muscles were no longer damaged. Unless you were looking for it, it would be something that a person would miss. But Elam saw it now and stood up beside her to touch it. The heat it gave off nearly took his breath away, and he turned her to look at him so that Casdon could see it closely as well.

"The slayer, the dragon slayer that you have here now, is trying to kill your beasts. His family has a long history with the death of the majestic ones. The reason that dragons have taken to hiding is because of his family. For generations they have been killing dragons for no other reason than to line their pockets. I did not know this until today. Izic told me before...before we...you know." He told her that they'd made love. With a short nod, Ariannona continued. "I was in mourning then. So many had been lost to the great war after the king and queen were slaughtered, and he caught me unaware. In a matter of days order was gone. Brothers were killing brothers. Houses were burnt to the ground. Nothing was ever going to be the same again, I feared. The body of neither of them were found for so long it was assumed that they might have escaped."

"My mother was hidden away with us, in the caves, and my father, he went down with the castle walls, we think." She told Casdon that that was what she knew to be true. "I forgot. You were there. When they lived."

"I was. They were good people. Better leaders than any one of us had ever had before." Elam asked her about the scar. "Someone gathered a small army, telling them that the queen still lived and that she needed to be killed before she came to avenge her mate's death. Many were not willing to leave their homes in the event that she returned. Even more of them packed up, deciding that to stay would mean their certain death. I remained to watch over the lady of the mountain so that no harm came to any of you."

"The slayer found the hiding space." She told him that he had not, but she did make him think that he had. "You were hurt, helping her then. Keeping the hatchlings safe, and thus myself and my brothers as well."

"I knew nothing of you. I only had just found the babies when I stumbled upon her dead body. I was trying to lead him away, you see. To make him think that I was the one that he hunted." Casdon asked her if she could shift. "Nay, but I could make him think that there was a large dragon he was seeing in the sky. And while I concentrated, his son, a young man, came up behind me and stabbed his pike though my back and left me there. Izic saved me by bringing one of the larger animals, a bear by the name of simply Bear, to come and free me from it and take me to Izic's pasture to heal."

"And he's been with you since." She nodded, and Elam sat down. She was deliciously naked and he felt his cock harden, but she picked up a shirt that was on the chair and he saw again the pain she had with simple movements. "You should take a long bath. The tub down the hall has jets and the hot water is endless. Then if you wish, there is a new hot tub out back that Casdon and I will ready for you when you come out."

"You mean to join me?" Her voice was nervous, her body stiff. He told her that she was going to bathe alone, and they had only just gotten the tub so it would take them time to fill it for her. "Oh. Well, okay then. I was.... Could you please leave the window open a bit? I'm expecting Izic to return soon with more information. And he might return while I'm bathing."

He could hear the relief in her voice. The embarrassment was apparent on her face and neck as well. Nodding once, he waited for Casdon to open the window and then leave by it as his dragon before handing her two towels, as well as a shirt of his and a pair of boxers that were Casdon's.

He was moving down the stairs when he thought that now that Ariannona was with them, Casdon would be wanting to sleep with them too. Instead of being embarrassed about what his brother might think, he asked Asher to enlarge the bedrooms and to make all the beds in the house larger by a great deal as well.

I have done the others. I thought since Casdon told us that the woman was his mate that she'd be yours as well. Let me know when to do your room. When you disappeared for so long, we all assumed you were working things out. He told him that they had, for now, and he told him Ariannona's name. *I know that name. It has a meaning. Let me think.... Ah yes, musical and artistic abilities. Sound judgement and responsibility for others. Do you suppose her parents knew that when they named her?*

I have no idea. Elam found Casdon staring at the instructions that had come with the tub. He didn't blame him much. After reading them in the city, he'd discovered that they were written for someone much smarter than he was. *Asher, about our hot tub. Can you help us out a little?*

Laughing, he watched as the tub not only unwrapped with unseen magic, but filled with hot water within seconds. He promised Asher he'd let him use it, but his brother told him he had one now as well. He and Casdon cleaned up the mess, neither of them saying a word about the naked woman bathing in their house.

Chapter 4

Ralph knew that he'd hit someone when he'd shot at the house. The scream that had accompanied his shot had made it clear that he'd hit a mark. He only hoped that it was the woman, and that he'd killed her before she told the men and women there what he was about. Ralph didn't want anyone trespassing on his work. The money was going to be all his. He was mad enough at her now to go and piss on her hopefully dead body.

He'd only just figured out what she'd done to his films. Ralph had no idea how she'd done it, but was sure that she had been the one to do it. All of his work, to capture a dragon on video, was ruined. No matter how many times he reprogramed his cameras and other equipment, it went back to the same loop, the same twenty-four hours that had nothing to show for it. Had it not rained the day before he'd sat down to look at the activity, he might never have known. But the bright sunny day and the night showing the same five deer coming out to play had him fast forwarding through several camera angles to figure it out.

"Damned woman." He moved about his camper trying to figure out what was missing there too. He had locked it up when he'd gone out, but now there seemed to be all sorts of things missing. And moved. His laptop had been placed on the floor, and all of his food had been tossed onto the ground. The only way for someone to have gotten in was to have crawled in the inch-wide space at the open window, and he knew that wasn't possible.

Sitting down, trying to get his head elsewhere for now, he looked at the map that was on his table. That too had given him some questions, but the answers weren't readily available for him. He brushed again at the tiny, what appeared to be footprints that walked around the entire map.

"Footprints, of all things. What the fuck is doing this?" He looked at the now closed window before going to the map again. "Ink stains. That's all it is, ink stains."

He studied the map. There was one area that he'd yet to check, about two thousand acres right in the middle of the valley, which he'd been avoiding. Ralph had gone there twice recently, and had been run off by a fucking bear of all things. And before that, he'd been so violently ill when he'd gotten there it had been all he could do to get back to his camper. He had no idea what would be making him sick, but figured it was some sort of toxic gas and that was why no one went there. Until a few days ago.

It was then that he'd not just seen the people living there, the new and old houses, but he'd seen that woman too. He'd not been able to go onto the nicely kept lawn. It had been surrounded by some sort of force. Not really a force field, though that had been what it felt like, but like he knew if he crossed over, he would die. Not be sick this time, but dead.

"Stupid notions." This, like the bear with the woman, had been something he had tried to erase from his mind. There was no way that she had commanded a bear to come after him that day. "I'm just tired. I need a long break."

And yes, he just realized, he was talking to himself. Again. He'd been doing that a lot lately as well, and tried to tell himself that he was just lonely and that he had been in the woods too long without another human to talk to.

He laid out his guns and tried to think what he should take with him tomorrow when he breached the area. Ralph was going to do it too. Go to the first home on the property and have himself a look around. If they were there, which he was hoping they wouldn't be, he'd ask to come in. If not, then he was going to have himself a look-see all on his own.

"I want that woman to know that she messed with the wrong guy." He knew that he was taking a chance going there. She might recognize him on some level, but he'd shaved his beard off last night and had had a go at his hair. He thought he looked enough different that in her hurt state, there was no way she would know it was the same man.

After he gathered up his weapons, gloves, and anything else he could fit on his person and in his backpack, he laid it near the door and went to his bedroom. After stripping down, he lay out on his bed and thought about what he'd been doing the last few years.

He'd been traveling around for nearly two years now. His wife of ten years had left him three months ago. Well, she'd filed for divorce three months ago. She claimed it was because he had spent all their money on this craziness. Not that he really cared anymore, and he was sure there were other things in the paperwork that he'd only just skimmed over. Like he'd not been home in months. That he'd been out of work longer than that.

Yes, he had spent the money, but as he'd worked for most of it, he felt that for once he shouldn't have to pay for nails to be done, streaks in her hair, and every new article of clothing that showed up in the window at the local expensive shops. He wanted to do this, and damn her for trying to tell him he was a fool for it.

Boots, socks, even sweaters in the summer would be purchased, stashed away, and only brought out when the weather was perfect. The kind that allowed a sweater to be worn but not a coat to cover it up. It was one of the many stupid things she did that bothered the fuck out of him. And now, as of a few months ago, he no longer had to care about her. There wasn't any need for support either, as she'd taken his home.

She had fifty—and he knew that it was a factual figure, not a guess—fifty pairs of shoes, each of varying colors but for the most part, the same shoe. And this did not count her boots, slippers, and sandals. Sandals, she told him once, had to be clean and new looking or they simply looked trashy. He told her at that point that he thought her trashy looking anyway. That statement didn't go over so well either, he thought with a laugh. And now here he was about to be famous. He wondered what she'd think of that, and found like the rest, he didn't give a crap about her.

"But she'll regret it now that she didn't give me a little more time when I asked for it. Once the bucks start rolling in for the shit I'm going to be able to sell off my dragon, the money won't be spent fast enough. Yes, sir, she is going to be shitting herself then." He reached behind his head for the list that he'd made up of the parts he was going to sell and their worth. He regretted not having his book that

Helena had given him, but he'd get that back as well when he went to the house.

Every single part of a dragon could be used. Not just for magic, because while he really didn't believe it, he knew that there were enough nutballs around that did. Even the scales were worth more than he made in a year's time. And they were so versatile, as were all the parts.

Selling them whole netted a great deal. Grinding them into a powder brought in more per ounce than gold did. Pieces of wings were nearly priceless, and if you were lucky enough to find a blue dragon or a red one, then the amount of money for each nearly tripled for some reason.

He hadn't a clue how many scales were on a dragon. The one that he'd killed had been pretty good sized. But without even knowing how big each one was, he was still clueless as to how many he could sell. Ralph was thinking five hundred would be a good number.

"I'm going to be fucking rich. And famous." He grinned as he rolled to his side. "Fucking amazingly rich and famous."

As he drifted off he heard something in the kitchen area. Peeking around the corner he didn't see anything, but he had left the light on. Getting up, grumbling about it the entire time, he entered the area and stood staring at the table he'd left the map on.

The footprints were still there, all around the area that he'd yet to go to. But in addition to it, there was what appeared to be blood and a crudely drawn picture of a man. He knew it was him without even getting close enough to see the clean-shaven face and the camo jacket that he always wore. Walking closer to it, he saw the words printed there.

Leave or die.

He sat down on his chair and stared at the map. When a cool breeze touched the back of his neck, he grabbed the gun off the table and shot four times in the general direction behind him.

He stared at the damage for several seconds before he realized what he was seeing. Christ, he was off his rocker. He rubbed his eyes several times before he looked again.

The footprints moved across the counter and to the now open window, like whatever it had been had walked in fresh ink. Or blood. Glass all over the counter as well as a broken curtain rod sat in the mess there. But it was the tiny little hat that had him shaking as he reached for it. It was blue, as blue as the sky was in the late evening. And so small that it didn't fit on the tip of his littlest finger when he'd picked it up.

He sat there, for how long he had no idea, but he kept staring at the mess he'd made and the hat. The hat that he was sure hadn't been there before. The little prints that seemed to just materialize, and which he knew there could have been no way for someone to get in and put them there.

And if they hadn't been there before, then where had they come from? Why were there prints on his map? Who had drawn a picture, a little bitty picture of him dead? And most of all, how the fuck had they gotten in to do all this shit?

~~~

I'm going to ask you something, and I don't want you to get mad at me. Well, not mad, but testy, like you have been lately. Elam looked at Casdon and nodded. His own mind was a mess of questions, but he wasn't even sure if he knew how to ask them. Or for that matter who the fuck he should ask. *Do you think that we did this really quickly? I mean, I know that as mates we're supposed to be right on top of things. You know, propagate the world and all. But there was an urgency there that I've never felt before. I didn't just want her, but I felt like I'd die if I didn't have her.*

Yes, yes. I feel that way as well. Like touching her isn't enough. Being near her just won't cut it. And we both seem to be all right with all of a sudden having a mate. Casdon said there was that too. *I've been thinking the same thing. I mean…I'm not saying that she tricked us into this relationship. But we went from not even wanting to think of a mate to picking out plate patterns.*

They weren't really, but he'd been thinking that was what they'd be doing next. He looked over at his brothers with their mates, both of them swollen with a child, and he wanted that too. But he wasn't sure that it was the right time, or this was the right woman. Something was wrong with this.

He looked at the castle now, trying to get his mind off Ariannona and onto anything else. There were things going on here too that he was concerned about. Things that he'd been thinking about all day but had kept it to himself. Not even going over it with Casdon, who up until now he'd never kept anything from. As Casdon moved away with more rubbish, he thought of what Asher had said just that morning.

"Someone has been down to the vault." He'd wanted to ask him how he knew but he'd continued before he could. "There are footprints in the dust and the place where the key is has been touched. No one has moved anything around that I can tell, but we've set some traps to find out who it might be."

"You think it's the slayer?" Asher had looked at Ariannona, then at him before he nodded. There had been a moment, just a small moment, when he'd thought his brother was trying to tell him something. But what, he had no idea. When Casdon returned, Elam sat down on the large stone that had yet to be placed with the other broken stones and tried to get his mind straight.

If he was honest with himself, all he could think about was going back to their house and fucking Ariannona again. None of them had left the bed for any longer than they'd had to since she'd moved in with them. This morning, however, Casdon had left them to go out flying. He said he'd needed to stretch his wings.

Elam wanted to lay there and just touch her. He'd been so relaxed that he must have fallen asleep. After making love to her all morning, he was exhausted and let sleep simply take him under. But the moment that he felt her mouth over his cock, he woke up with a roar and his hand holding her to him.

"Christ, yes." Elam had watched her bob her head up and down over him for several minutes, just fucking her slowly, not wanting to rush anything. And when she touched her fingers to his balls, then cupped them in her hand, he sat up quickly and felt his cock empty inside of her.

His heart had been pounding so hard that he was sure that he was going to have a stroke. His body, no longer fully aroused, felt like he'd been given a gift...not just with the sex, but with her as well. Elam thought he sounded sappy when he thought about it later. But then she moved, her body so close to his that he could smell her heat, and he wanted to take her again. Taste her as she flooded his mouth with all that she was.

"My turn."

Ariannona nodded, and when she lay down beside him he moved down her body, tasting any part of her he could until he got to her pussy. Christ, even the smell of her now could make him hard, and he adjusted his cock through his pants as he thought about eating her.

She always let him know either by coming or screaming out her release that she was enjoying herself. Twice while he'd eaten at her this morning, he paused to watch her play with her breasts, squeezing her nipples until they were as pink as her nether lips. But when she begged him to fuck her, to slam his cock into her, he could no more not do that than he could have not come inside her.

"You're very hot." Her nod had him laughing. Taking her breast into his mouth, he had suckled it hard, then chewed on her nipple as he teased her pussy with the crown of his cock. "Do you want me?"

"Yes. Oh yes, please. All of you." When he slid into her, closing his eyes against the onslaught of pleasure, she wrapped her legs around him tight enough that with each of his strokes, she moaned. "Elam, I'm coming. Oh yes, I'm coming."

He pounded her through her climax, his own body so close that he hurt with it. And when she bit down on his shoulder, he cried out, his entire body bowing back almost double as he came as hard as he'd ever come before in his entire life.

"Elam?" He looked at her, standing there before him now, and tried to get the urge to take her against the closest hard surface that he could find out of his mind. When she took a step back from him, Elam wasn't sure what he was going to do, but he stood up and moved toward her. "Don't touch me."

"I didn't hurt you." She said she knew that, but didn't want him to touch her. "Why not? Am I suddenly not good enough for you? You only want me when we're behind closed doors where no one can figure out that we're fucking? Or have you finally had your fill of me? Are you moving on to some other sap?"

He didn't know why he'd said that, but the slap to his face made him feel justified for some reason, and when he lashed out at her again, she turned and left. Then she just disappeared. As he sat back down, not sure what the fuck had just happened, Asher jerked him up from the rock and knocked him back on his ass with his fist. Within seconds, it was a free for all, and they were all fighting like animals.

The shrill whistle had him stop in mid punch to Gideon. Asher had Simeon down and was beating the shit out of him, and the rest of them were fairing no better. But they all stopped and stared at Essie when she whistled again.

"Now, we're going to be grown adults about this." Asher growled low, and Essie turned to him. "Did you not understand me? I said that we're going to be adults. Let him go."

"He hit me."

She took a step toward Asher, and he let Simeon drop to the ground. The dragons, all of them, had been fighting as well, but they'd taken it to the sky and were landing now. Essie, their queen, had spoken. His dad was sitting on the same stone he'd been on, but he was smiling, not arguing with anyone.

"As I was saying. Would someone like to tell me what the fuck is going on? You have been snapping and biting at one another for two days, and I will not stand for it any longer." No one moved, but it did occur to Elam that he'd been short with everyone, not just Ariannona. "I'm waiting."

"Since she's been here." Everyone turned and looked at him and he felt stupid. "What I meant was, since Ariannona got here, I've not been able to be in the room with anyone but her without wanting to rip some throats out."

"I noticed that too. Not just on Elam here, but all of you." His dad looked at him. "But you and Casdon, you got no problem with your mate. Asher? Jed? You mad at your mates too?"

"No. Just...everything about these guys makes me want to...hurt them." His dad nodded and looked at Essie, asking her if she was mad all the time too.

"No. I'm pissed off because this shit is going on, but I'm not wanting to kill anyone."

Elam sat down on the ground and felt sick to his stomach. It was profound, the feeling, like he was going to puke and turn his belly out while doing it. When he felt a cool hand on his face, he put his hand over it and knew it was Ariannona.

"What are you doing to us?" She stepped back from him as if he'd slapped her. "I'm sorry. I don't know what's wrong with me, and it's only been since you've been here. It has to be you. You're doing this."

"You think I've put some sort of spell on you or something? That I've come here to kill you off?" He nodded, then leaned over and did empty his gut. When he rolled to his back, she was on his chest then and holding his head with her hands. "Look at me."

"I'm sick." She said that she knew that. "I can't...what's wrong with me? I feel like I'm dying."

"You are." As he rolled to his side again, knocking her off, he felt like he was throwing up all the way from his toes. And when he glanced up, he saw that Casdon was sick too, his dragon lying on the grass with his brothers all around him.

Elam closed his eyes only to have someone yelling at him to open them. It was Ariannona again, but she was so out of focus for him that he was sick all over. Twice she screamed at him to wake, and both times he couldn't do it without a great deal of effort. Finally, he gave up and let his body slip away.

Chills, then fire, racked his body. One minute he was so cold that he was sure he'd been put in the freezer. The next he was so hot that he asked if Casdon was trying to kill him. At least he thought he had. His mind was as fuzzy as his body hurt.

People came and went in his vision. His mom, then dad was there. Someone was holding his hand. Then another time he was being dangled from one of the dragon's claws. He felt his skin crawl with bugs, flaying his skin off him as they ate their way to his heart. He heard someone saying his name, but he shied away from it, knowing that danger was there for him.

"Elam." He looked then, his body so weak that he could no longer shiver. His head was sick with trying to think, and he knew that he was as close to dying as he'd ever been. "Elam, can you hear me?"

"Yes." He felt the pain in his throat, like a torch had been set to it and was still burning brightly. "I hurt."

"I know you do. I'm trying to fix it." He nodded once, then stopped. It was too hard to move, much less be sick again because of it. "Do you know who I am? Can you see me?"

"Mom." He had no idea why he knew it was her, but he felt a little better knowing that she was coming for him at his death. "I'm so sorry about the cookie jar. I wanted to replace it, but you got sick."

"I did. But I knew that you'd had help in breaking it." He nodded again and felt his belly burn again. "Don't move. I'm looking you over. My goodness, child, why are you still alive? Just die already."

That made him stop and think; even through the pain he knew that wasn't right. He wanted to ask her if she thought him ready to pass over, but he felt her touch on his skin and pulled away from it. When he opened his eyes, even for the briefest of moments, he saw Ariannona there.

"That was you. You made me think that my mother would say that I should just die." She shook her head and he could see the tears on her face. "She's looking me over and said I should die already. But it wasn't her. It was you. All this time, it was you."

He closed his eyes again and felt another touch to his brow. Cold and hateful, Elam tried to get away from it. On some level he knew that he was hurting someone, and he thought that it might be someone important to him. But he was sick again and tried to shut the pain off by letting himself slip away. The next time he woke he was being tied down, or so his fevered mind thought.

Elam lashed out at the person trying to hold him. He had no idea what they thought they were doing, and he wanted to tell them to just let him die. His magic was useless now. He was too weak to call on it, and even if he did have the ability to, he had no idea what he was supposed to do.

"Elam?"

He didn't answer the voice this time. He knew that whoever it was, they were not going to be helping him. He was tired. Too tired to think any more. As he drifted off, he heard a voice, low and full of authority.

"Elam Benson, you'll pay attention to me right now." The king. Elam had no clue how he'd known who it was, but he was sure that it was the old king. "You going to let my son die too? You want your mate to be alone? You cannot die, do you hear me? A great deal is depending on the two of you getting better."

"I'm sick and no one cares." The king laughed and Elam asked him why that was funny. "You have been here, lying about in this, for five days now, and no one has left your side but for moments. No one cares, my foot. Get up from this pity party."

A peace came over him. The touch to his face was no longer scary but comforting. As he let his body go, not in death as he'd wished for but in sleep, he wondered if Casdon was getting better too.

"You hurt her. You'll have to fix this if you wish to move on in this world." He said he didn't want anyone in his life; it was fine the way it was. "And having no children is fine with you? Not having someone to love you and Casdon, no matter what, that's good as well? You'll live a very sorry, sad life, Elam, if you do not get your head out of your ass."

Chapter 5

Ariannona adjusted herself on the chair again. There simply wasn't any comfortable way to sit in the chair, especially not after sitting there for nearly a week. When she'd had enough, Ariannona snapped her fingers and moved deeper into the chair she'd conjured. Izic laughed at her when she sighed heavily

"You should have done that days ago, mistress. I did tell you that it was most uncomfortable to even look at." She nodded and looked over at the two men on the bed. Elam's fever had broken last night, Casdon's the day before. Both men had been too near death for her to want to think about.

"Have you told the others what has poisoned them?" Ariannona shook her head. She said she was afraid to. "The young master, he blamed you for this. He does not know yet that he was right."

"None of them do. I had no idea either until I moved into their bodies while they slept to see how I could fix this. I saw it in his mind, Elam's. He hates me and all that I stand for in his life." Izic nodded and came to sit on the arm of the chair beside her. "They're not going to be happy that I did this to them. I could have killed them all. But I will take care of it."

"You had no way of knowing either, mistress. It was not explained to you that it would harm them." Ariannona said nothing but watched the two men in slumber. They would be all right now, and once they were awake and she told them what had happened, they'd tell her to leave. Not that she wasn't going to go anyway, but it might make her feel better should they tell her to go. She was tucking memories in her heart, or what was left of it, to look at later.

When Essie came in and sat across the room from her, Ariannona thought it was well past time to explain things. If she had her leave now, she'd not have to endure the pain of one of these men telling her to get out and to never return.

"The blue rose, have you heard of it?" Without looking in her direction, Ariannona explained to her when Essie said that she'd not. "It's of my design. I bred it to be my signature flower, I guess. When the king and queen changed me, gave me what powers they could, I was in nothing more than rags and decided that I wanted to stand out. The white of my hair, it came with the magic. I think that I was showing off. No, I know that I was. They, the great king and queen of the kingdom, had given me a part of themselves."

"Are you trying to tell me that this is an allergic reaction to a rose that you made?" Ariannona said something like that, but not purely. "I want you to explain that to me then. Why a flower that you made has anything to do about any of this. They were about dead, and something like that cannot kill men like these. They're immortal. They have to have their heads removed to be killed."

"Most of the time, yes. But I was wearing the blue rose.... Let me start at the first. King Anthony was upset that night. I think he was stressed out. I know that his lady wife had just given birth that morning, and perhaps he was a little on edge. When he spoke to me, he told me that he had a favor for me to do. And I, of course, wanted answers before I would agree and.... Well, you understand."

"Yes. I think I do. He was in a hurry as well, I would bet. It's my understanding, from the timeline you have mentioned that they were close to being murdered. And they knew it." Ariannona said it was three days later that the castle came down. "And this favor, it was to come and give this whatever to Casdon, and they set you up as his and Elam's mate."

"The mate part I wasn't aware of. I'm pretty sure they might have, but they didn't tell me anything about it. More than likely because they thought I'd not do as they asked. But when they touched me, the two of them at the same time, I got a little more than they meant to give me, I think. Not only did I know where the children were, but I knew that Sally and Jacob would have six sons, and that Jacob would be brought from his entombment to be with his boys. Sally is there too...I'm not sure how, but she's dimmer in my thoughts about them, like maybe they weren't quite sure what part she played later in their lives. I'm not sure how, but I knew it." Essie asked if Sally was going to be freed from the grave. "I don't know for sure."

"Okay, they gave you magic, and a great deal of it." Ariannona said that they'd not given her all of it, but she'd grown into some of it as well. "Much like Caroline did, with age and experience grows more magic."

"Yes. That's it. But unlike Caroline, I'm not either white or black, so I wasn't able to take from the ones that I killed. And I did have to kill a great many witches to survive." Ariannona had no idea why, but she'd expected Essie to be horrified at what she'd said. But instead, she asked her to go on, like it had not been that big of a revelation. "The blue rose. It was the only colored flower that I wanted to feel on my person. The royal chambers where we were that night were of the richest blues and purples. That might have been the reason. Really after all this time, I'm not sure anymore."

"And you're telling me that this flower is the thing that felled these two men." Ariannona nodded, then shook her head. "Yes, that is very helpful."

"After I left the castle that night, I ran into Helena. She was evil, even then, but there was something about her that made me more than fearful. It made my skin crawl. When she saw me coming from the castle keep that night, she asked me what I had been doing there. I told her, stupidly, I now see, that it was none of her business. She hit me, with a cane that she sometimes used when she was trying to make people see things her way. And with the power of the king and queen still buzzing along my skin, I wanted to kill her. My anger was so strong that it was everything I could do not to use my newfound power and end her miserable life. But I'd been told, several times, not to interfere. And I had a feeling that something she was doing or about to do would be why I was asked to come to see them." Ariannona looked at the two men, then back out the window. She'd caused this, the men in her life to be so ill. "The flower was...I would guess you'd think it was vanity on my part. They had changed me, you see. Given me a great deal, but I knew even then that they'd taken as well. And when she saw it, the only color on my body, she...."

She remembered it like it had only just happened. That she'd been hurt not just by her cane, but by her magic as well. But she'd done nothing. Held onto her temper because she had an idea that things were not as they seemed. And the meeting with the king and queen was something that she could not share. Especially not with Helena.

"What did she do to you, Ariannona?" *What didn't she do to me would have been a better question*, she thought, but Ariannona moved back to the chair and sat down. "She cursed you."

"Yes. And these men in a way. The rose that I'd made for me made her angry for some reason. Its purity, she said, but I think it was more. Like perhaps she thought that it had been a gift from them. But she cursed me, for whatever her reasons were, because of it. 'Your blood is poison. Your heart will be black. Until you meet a man that trusts you fully, gives you his heart fully, you will kill what you love.' Then she plucked the flower from my chest and blew over it, turning it as black as her own heart. She returned it to me and the thorn pricked my finger, sealing the deal, I guess." She stood up then and moved to the door. There wasn't anything else she could do here. "I was going to wait to tell them goodbye, but I think this is better, don't you? To leave while.... None of them trust me, and they never have. The arguments will stop now. The two of them will be getting better quickly now that...well, once I'm gone. My inability to have them trust me for whatever reason is the reason they were near dead."

"What did the king give you to give to Casdon? How did it save him that night?" She smiled then at Essie. Of course she'd want to know that. "I understand that you feel you must go. But the gift, what was it? Will they be harmed by it as well?"

"No harm will come to any of them now, not from me or from anything else. Casdon and the rest of you will now be able to take iron into your body. Before, as a magical creature, iron would kill, as I'm sure you know. Even the dragons that come here, each of them you touch, they will survive like they couldn't before. I think...it's what made them so weak, the king and queen, giving me this to share with their sons." Essie asked her why Casdon, and Ariannona laughed before answering her. "You may not believe it, but the lady queen thought him to have the purest of hearts."

As she made her way out of the house she pulled shadows around her. It was not that she was sneaking out or that she thought anyone would try and stop her. Ariannona simply did not want to speak to any of them, or to hear them tell her to leave. This way, she figured, she'd leave with just a little of her heart. Shattered as it was.

"My lady." Izic landed on her shoulder as she continued to walk across the fields. As they made their way to the outer skirts of the land and the magic, she felt her body begin to change again. Magic left her. Not a great deal, but it was enough to make her stumble slightly. And even her clothing, white still even after all these centuries, began to fade; the color, so brilliant before now, was graying. "You will die now? Your love for them, it cannot hold you here forever?"

"No, I don't believe so." He said nothing to her but stayed with her as they made their way to their home. "When I pass, would you do me a favor, my friend? Go to the dragon savior and live among them. I wish for you to be safe from harm. Even if you do not want to live where they see you, you will be safe on the land of the king, I think."

"I shall do this only because you have asked me so prettily." She could hear the pain in his voice and felt it all the way to her broken heart. "I will find me a mate, have children, and name them all for you. Will that make you smile, my lady?"

"Nay, your lady wife will be most upset with you. You should name them for her. Not someone who nearly killed the saviors of our creatures." He said nothing, but she could feel his pain like her own. "Izic, I have another favor to ask of you. A small one, but one I would take to my heart as I die. Would you please not tell them? Not let them know my fate or what has become of me?"

"You wish me not to tell them of your death?" She nodded, the tears blinding her for a few moments, her pain so great that she leaned against the tree. "My mistress, you love them. Why do you leave them?"

"I must, as you know. I hurt them. Yes, they did not trust me as they should, but I have given them no reason to do so. I have been tainted and they paid the price." If he answered her, she didn't know. "Will you make me this promise?"

"Yes, mistress, I give you my word. I shall not tell anyone living of your death, my lady." She started to ask him what he meant by that but didn't. "When you pass, I will call to the earth to make a great faerie circle that will rival even that of the great dragon, Dawod. Humans will stand over it, marveling at such a miracle of life, and wonder a great deal who had done such a thing."

"Thank you." She knew that he had no power to do such a thing, but was touched to her toes that he'd said it. "Tell me what you know of the slayer. Perhaps we can do more harm to him before it's time so that they might heal just a little more. The castle, it will need to be completed soon. And once it is, the magic will be much stronger there."

As he told her what he knew, what he'd done, she laid down on her pallet of soft down and cotton. It was the one thing that she'd brought with her when she'd come here...the soft cotton to sleep upon. A pillow made of the softest material, too.

"He is most upset with me. Well, not me but what he has found. I only stepped in the pen flow for a moment and took only a step or two. But I so loved how it looked that I made several more tips to the well of it. The ink is most smelly, by the way. I loved how it made me appear to be all over his house, but I suppose in a way that I was. But only on the counter did I leave my prints. It was—" She only said his name and it brought him back to what she'd asked of him. "The slayer has a weak mind, easy to turn. I think that will be useful in the future in dealing with him."

As her magic depleted, much faster than she thought it would have, she plotted and planned with Izic. Keeping him on task was harder than she thought it should have been, but they got it done. When she could no longer hold her head up, she closed her eyes and let sleep take her. Tomorrow she'd have to make notes to have Izic take to the new queen. She, Ariannona knew, trusted her enough to listen to him.

~~~

Elam lay as still as he could. He hurt, but he knew that for some reason he wasn't going to be sick again. And even though his belly felt a little tense, he thought it was just empty and not sick that made him feel this way. He looked over at Asher when he said his name.

"You're well now?" He said that he thought he might be. "Good. I'm so pissed off at you right now that I could gladly pull you from that bed and beat you until you cannot walk again."

"Because I got sick?" Asher said nothing but got up to pace. His body was hard, his forehead furrowed in concentration, and each step looked as if he were trying his best to break the board beneath him. "Perhaps you'd be in a better mood had I died. I'm sure that whatever befell me will come back to finish the job."

"You don't trust her. Even though twice she has saved Casdon, and now you, you have no trust for her." He asked him what he was talking about. "Ariannona. You might love her, but that's all you have for her."

"I don't understand what you're talking about." Elam sat up. His body was weak but not rebelling any longer. "Where is she? I thought she'd be here. With me. And where is Casdon?"

"Casdon has taken to the skies. He said that he'd not return because of what he has done. The two of you should be beaten." Elam swung his legs over the side of the bed and sat there while the room seemed to settle around him. "I'm not just blaming you that she's gone. We all had a part in her leaving us. But I think I can lay even our part in her being gone at yours and Casdon's feet."

"Would you please explain what the fuck you are talking about? Just one thing at a time though. I'm not...I feel a little weird." Asher sat down in front of him and told him he was sorry, but no less pissed at him. "So am I. I don't know what happened, but I'd like for you to start with what happened to Casdon and I."

"There was a curse. One that was put on Ariannona right after she talked to the king and queen. Helena the black again." Elam nodded but held his head in his hands as he asked Asher to continue. "It's a curse that says that her blood is poison to the one that she loves. That so long as he doesn't trust her, she will end up killing him. You and Casdon in this case. I'm assuming, since it's stopped since she left here, that us fighting was part of it too. That since the rest of us didn't take her blood the curse would have us kill each other, and not die of blood poisoning as it seemed to be doing to you and Casdon."

"I trust her." Asher only glared at him. "All right, I didn't, but I had good reason not to. And you didn't either, by your own admission. Or you wouldn't have gotten a part of it."

"And this reason for the lack of trust, what is it? And I will readily admit that I didn't trust her. Not fully. And I think now that it was because you and Casdon didn't. You cast doubt over her and we were all feeding on it. Except Dad and Grandda. Neither of them were affected by it. Neither were the women. I guess it was just us, mostly the two of you, that had a problem with her."

Elam tried to think. She was gone? Why not talk to him about it? Let him explain. But he could answer that almost right away. Because she figured that they wouldn't have listened to her explanation. And he more than likely wouldn't have.

"It was so fast, this thing between us, don't you think? Casdon and I, we talked about it between the two of us. Even when he met her, out on the meadows, he said that he could barely contain himself not to touch her, taste her. And when she came here...." Elam sat there thinking about the chain of events that had brought them to this point. "We had no desire to have a mate. I mean, none. We were talking before she arrived that we were happy to be together, live our lives as we wanted." Feeling stronger now, he stood up and sat on the chair instead of the bed. He felt a kind of heartbreak and rubbed his hand over the injured muscle. "Then as soon as she came to us, we were sappy and our lives...just seemed to turn upside down. It was as if she'd made us feel like that, like we wanted her in our lives rather than her just simply being our mate. Do you understand?"

"You fucking moron. So you just decided that you'd fuck her but not give her the one thing in the world that people need to survive." He asked him if he meant love. "Love was there, Elam. You and Casdon loved her very much, I think. But you never fully gave her the part of you that she gave you. Trust, and without trust, love simply cannot grow. It'll wither and die, much like it did for the three of you."

"I didn't think it was real. I honestly think that she's done something to us. Or the king has to make us have these...these overwhelming feelings for her. Feelings that just aren't real." Asher stood up and moved to the door. "What do you want me to do, Asher? Go find her? Tell her that I'm sorry? That I do trust her to have her come back here?"

"Nay, you have lied to her enough, I think. Telling her that falsehood would only make it worse." Elam watched Asher, thinking this was the stupidest thing he'd ever had happen to him. "And you should know that Essie thinks that Ariannona's going to die. Alone and not long from now. Not because of you, or I should despise you, but because she has fulfilled the favor and arrangement that she made before coming here. After this, I'm sure she feels that her promise to the king and queen of before is finished and she has nothing left to live for." Then he was gone.

Elam sat there, not sure what he was supposed to do now. He felt like a lot of his heart had been damaged, and reached out to Casdon to see if...maybe he would have some good news for him. But the connection seemed blocked. Like he too was mad at him.

Elam knew that he loved her. Even now he knew that. But the reasons he didn't trust her were his own. As he'd told Asher, things had progressed much too fast for him, and he was afraid of it. Maybe instead of not trusting her, he was afraid of her.

"Not her. Just this thing." He got up to go to the bathroom to shower. He was looking in the mirror at himself when something else occurred to him. Thoughts of what he'd been thinking while sick.

Someone had...the king had been there, yelling at him for what he'd done. That he should fix this so that the king's son and Elam could live. Then the king was ordering him about as if he were there and could act upon his threats. He remembered thoughts, snatches of dreams too, of living alone, dying the same way. Not even with Casdon beside him. As he scrubbed all the sweat and sickness off him, Elam wondered if that was part of the curse too, to have nothing save himself to live with. Standing under the hot spray, he thought of his mother for some reason and what she'd meant to him.

Love. It had been the kind of love that you could bask in. Every day she told them all that she loved them. Not just verbally but with everything she did. Cooked them their favorite meals, gave them a gentle and sometimes a not so gentle touch when they needed it. Even when she was cross with them, she never made them feel that she didn't love them. And when they told her something, no matter what it was, she would give them the most honest answer she had.

As he was pulling on his clothing, his need to see his mom overwhelming, he thought of the last time he'd been to the little cemetery, and it was so distant that he felt badly about it. He used to go there every time he came home. Cleaned the area, planted fresh flowers for her. Since he'd been home this time, he'd not been there once. Life, it seemed, had gotten in the way.

Making his way to the little area, he was disappointed to see his dad there, talking to his mate.

"Ah son, we were just talking about you." He looked at his dad, then at the headstone. "She talks to me. Every day when I come here, I tell her about my day, about you boys. I love her very much. I know that you all do as well, but...well, she was my world and I miss her more and more daily."

Elam sat down on the grass beside his mother's grave and plucked two patches of weeds from the ground, and without thought, he asked the lady of the earth to forgive him, please. He wanted to talk to his mom, but felt that maybe his dad could help him since she was gone from him. Perhaps this was why he'd wanted to come here, knowing that his father might be here.

"Everything is all messed up at home. Casdon is gone and says he's never to return. I've tried to contact him, to talk to him, but he's blocking me. And I don't trust Ariannona." Dad said that he'd heard that. "I love her. That much I'm sure of, but I don't trust her. And now she's left because of that. Asher is pissed off too, that I ran her off somehow by not giving her my heart and my trust."

"It got you better, her leaving you alone to be pitiful." He asked Dad what he meant. "The curse. She left you so you and the rest of them could get better. And by the way, you can't have love if you don't have trust too. It's like saying you have pie when you got no crust. All you got is a bowl of fruit and nothing else. Not even prettying it up with some homemade ice-cream can make it a pie. Trust and love, they're the same thing."

"I'm beginning to think perhaps I've made a mistake." His dad only nodded. "While I was ill, I saw the king there. And he told me to buck up and get better. He told me that I was going to kill his son with my mistake. I think he meant Ariannona, but I can't change my mind on this. I think she put a spell on us to make us love her. Or the king did. However it came to be, we were tricked."

"The king, he would have taken you to the shed, the both of you. Casdon and you. But to your statement about him. In this dream of yours, you get your bottom kicked by a dead king and come out to talk to your equally dead mother. You don't even trust the living to tell you you're a fool, do you?" He said that wasn't fair. "Your mother would have been very upset with the two of you. She loved you enough to die for you. Me too. You boys, all of you, meant more to us than our own lives. And I knew that should anything happen to any of you...well, we'd just not want to go on living."

"Why?" His dad asked him what he meant. "Why did you love us that much? I mean, I understand that you're my father and she's my mom, but why did you love us so much that you gave up everything to keep us?"

"It wasn't any kind of hardship if that's what you're thinking." He said it wasn't. "Love you? I guess because you were a part of us that we'd given life too. Some of our hearts were a part of each of you. Our skin and blood. Even our brains, they made up what you were too. But that don't explain the love, I guess. We seen plenty of people who gave the same bits of themselves to make a baby and didn't love it."

"You mean Essie." He nodded. "She was tricked into being with us too. Like Lindsey. The bits and pieces as you call them, they were preordained...someone manipulated the fates for them to be made or born to come to us. Same with Ariannona."

"So, you don't trust the woman that was meant for you because someone fixed it up so that you could meet." Elam wasn't sure that was it, but didn't answer his dad. "You little shit. I cannot believe.... You throw away the best thing in the world because.... What do you think would have happened to you if that good king had not gotten it into his head to have me and your mother come together? You'd not be here, right now, making me mad enough to want to paddle you but good."

"Dad, I didn't—"

"'Course you didn't think, if that was what you were gonna say. If you had you'd have taken care not to say those things." He tried again. "Don't you even talk to me right now. You just said to me that you think that me and your mother's love and happiness wasn't good enough for you. That because someone had blessed us with the foresight to bring the two of us together to be happy, that it's not trustworthy."

His dad looked at the headstone and closed his eyes. He knew, Elam knew as surely as he was sitting there, that his dad was talking to his mom, and Elam felt a loss so profound that he hurt with it. His breaths were painful to bring in and out of his body because he'd hurt the one person in the world that he loved more than anything.

"Your momma said to tell you that Ariannona, she's dying. That her friend told her today that Ariannona would not make it through the night." Elam stood up and his dad told him to sit. "Your momma also said that she's disappointed in you as well. That she's almost ashamed to think that you would think things like that. That the fates don't have a say in everything you do."

"It happened so fast." His dad nodded but said nothing. "How was I supposed to feel when everything that I had no idea that I ever wanted was thrown in my lap? That I'd feel this way about a woman only after a few minutes?"

"Fast? Let me tell you about fast, son. The night I met the king, he had summoned me to his chamber and he sat me upon his lady wife's chair to speak to me. He knew I was armed. Had me a knife not just in my pocket by my hip, but in my boot as well. But he wanted me close to him, trusted me not to harm him when I could see he was near death himself." Elam sat down and listened to his father. "He never mentioned me falling in love with the woman I was to have children with. Never told me that I'd be as happy a man as I'd ever hoped to be with the way my children were born to us. Love...it never entered my mind that I'd not love this woman that walked beside me, ran from the death and destruction that would fell a kingdom. As soon as I took her hand in mine, held it while I helped her over fallen trees and stones, I knew then that she was going to be the love of my life. Even Elbert knew that I'd never harm her, trusted me to this day with his child. To love her, care for her in ways that, as her father, he never could. And you tell me after a few minutes the love that you felt for a woman meant for you was untrustful. I'm surely ashamed of you, Elam. I am at that."

As his dad left him there, got up and just walked away, Elma looked at his mother's marker and spoke to her. Tears streamed down his face when his dad's words worked their way into his already bruised and battered heart.

Chapter 6

"I'm a fool." Casdon didn't feel any better about his declaration saying it aloud in the empty cave, but he started this and now he was going to finish it. "Mom, I don't know what I was thinking to be so upset with her. It wasn't her fault that someone shoved her at us."

That wasn't right either. No one had shoved her anywhere. In fact, he'd bet that if anyone tried, they'd be dead about now. He got up to pace the cavern where his mom lay. She was there, lying next to his shell along with his brothers, keeping them as safe as she could have done. Even after her death she continued to protect them.

"You sent her to us. Why? The magic? Essie told me what the gift was that you gave us, and how much it cost you to do so. Is that why you died? Giving me something that would save my life and that of Elam when the time came?" He heard a soft sound and knew that he was hearing things. There wasn't any way that he heard someone tell him to grow up. "Mom, I'm afraid of what I've done."

And he was too…ashamed and afraid. He'd been a fool, as he'd said, but worse than that, he'd been hurtful to someone. Someone he was sure was going to die. And that would be the worst tragedy of all.

"I've been looking for her for hours. And not only do I have no idea where she might be, but I've no way of contacting her. It's as if she is simply gone from this earth." He didn't want to think about what that might mean for her. Or for him. She was dead, he knew it, and it hurt him in more ways than just his body. Casdon thought his heart would never be the same. He heard something again and looked around the chamber. When he realized he was alone, he looked at his mom again. "I think I talked Elam into not trusting her. It was my questions that gave his seeds of doubt root. I should have…I was going to say kept my mouth shut, but that's not it either. I should have trusted myself and her in this."

He got up to pace and stopped when he'd taken three or four turns. Putting his hand onto the cold stone, he felt the first stirrings of life beyond it. The feeling that, if he wanted to dig through the stone, he could find the life that was there, just going about their lives as if he'd not just ruined his.

"When I was a small boy, living here with Elam and the rest of them, I could never understand why it was so important for us to never leave the land. I knew that I was a part of Elam, our bodies would merge all the time, but the fact that it seemed to me that we were trapped here was a feeling that I'd not understood." Not trusted, his mind said to him. "So I took a walk, thinking that once I was off the land I could come back and tell them all what I'd found. I'd be considered this great adventurer and all would hail me."

It had been his dream for days after he'd thought about it. He'd even packed him a meal or two and gotten a blanket, so he could stay the night somewhere. Casdon had sat at the table that morning thinking how things would be different when he returned. That everyone would treat him like a king. The morning he'd deemed to be the first day of his life had nearly been the last.

"There were four men out that day. All of them were hunters…I saw the bows and arrows they had. The knives that hung low on their belts, and even the fur, bloodied and fresh, on their backs from their catch. I wasn't really afraid of them. I was just a kid, I thought. No harm to them. I thought I'd stepped off the land not ten minutes before, so I stayed hidden." Casdon closed his eyes, thinking of the events that had changed him so much that day. "The first man saw me and he grinned. At the time, I thought I was safe; they were men, I was but a child. And I was a dragon too should I need him. What harm could they do to one such as me? But as they drew closer, their blades now drawn, I took steps back. Too quickly and clumsily. I knew then that they only wanted to murder me. Not because of me being part dragon, but because I was alone and they were bigger."

He'd fallen on his ass. The men loomed over him and he knew that he was going to have his head removed. The men, taller and stronger than him, were going to end his life and no one would be the wiser. All his adventures had gotten him, he remembered thinking, was to die here in the other land with no one to mourn him.

"Something came out of nowhere. I had no idea at the time what it was or who. But as soon as the men fell back, I got up and ran all the way back to the house and to my room." He smiled then, thinking how terrified he'd been and that he'd not even used his dragon. "I wasn't off the land as I had thought. Days later I took Elam out there with me...for moral support, I guess...and realized that I'd been about an inch, just a mere inch, from stepping onto land that wasn't our own. Where I fell and where the men had been wasn't the same property."

He knew later what had come for him. Elbert, as his dog. He'd been following close behind him, knowing, he told him later, that he was up to no good. Casdon didn't think he ever told Sally or Jacob. Had he done so, Casdon would have been in trouble, more than likely would have taken his first trip to the dreaded wood shed. He told Elam a few days later, when he didn't feel like the world was coming to get him.

Elam had made him promise that he'd never do anything like that again. Never leave him. He'd been so afraid that he'd told him he wasn't going to. He'd told him that he knew that the two of them were connected, but even if they weren't, he loved him with all that he was and he'd not want to live without him there. Casdon had made and kept that promise.

He talked to his mom for another few hours, telling her things about his life, the woman that he'd hurt, and how much he wished he could find her. As he was leaving the deep cavern, a small brownie buzzed his head and he nearly fell back trying to dodge him. It was Ariannona's friend, and Casdon was glad to see him.

"You must come with me." He said that he was going to look for Ariannona. "Yes. Good. But I must speak with...with the queen. Come and.... You will watch over me so that I come to no harm."

He started to turn him down. He had to leave now before it got too much darker, but the urgency of the little guy's voice, the posture of his body, made Casdon go back down the long deep corridor again. As they reached his mom's body, the little brownie — he thought his name was Izic — told him to come closer.

"I do not wish for harm to come to me." Casdon looked around and asked him who he thought was going to hurt him here. "You have no idea. But I have made a promise. And I must keep it or she will be most upset with me."

The word promise made him stay. A lot of those had been broken of late, and he didn't want to be responsible for breaking another. So he knelt down on his knees to watch for the little Izic, the friend of his love.

"I have been made to promise not to say a word about her illness and where she is." Izic looked at him and told him to not listen. After nodding, Izic turned to Casdon's mom and started to yell at the top of his lungs. "I have made a promise not to tell a living soul where the fallen witch is. Nor to tell anyone that she lay dying."

"She's dying? Do you know where?" Izic told him to be quiet and not to listen. "And how do you propose I do that when...? Ah, I see. Yes, tell my mother all you know and I won't listen."

Izic glared at him, but there was a twinkle in his eyes as he continued. "Her heart is broken, and I fear that if someone doesn't come to save her, all will be lost. And a lost love is the worst kind of loss, if you ask me." He glared at him again, this time without the spark in his eyes. Unless you counted the anger he saw there. Izic then looked back at the fallen queen. "She is in the north pasture near the lake. I have had the glen faeries watch over her, but I fear that they are too stupid to do a good job. The other brownies, they're trying, but they do not love her as I do."

"I love her." Izic told him to hush. "Yes, I'm sorry. But I do love her. Very much. She's wonderful, and I don't wish for her to die."

"She said you have no trust of her heart." He said that he was wrong to think that way. "Yes, you were. Her heart is as pure as the day you took her. Did she not, after all these centuries on this earth, trust you with something so wonderful as all that she is? And like the other, you tossed it back at her as if it were nothing but dirty wash. Shame on you, Casdon, son of Anthony and Eve, king and queen of dragons."

"My heart hurts when I think of all the things that I've done to her. That the two of us—Elam and I—did to her. She is giving and unselfish with her heart and I...we trampled it." Izic said that they had, him and Elam. "I want you to take me to her please. I want to make sure she's all right and bring her back into my life."

"You cannot save her alone. There are the two of you." Casdon nodded and said he'd find Elam. "He searches for you now, so that the two of you can find her. His mother, she is a good listener too."

Casdon laughed. The guy had gotten around the promise by telling not just his mom but Sally as well. As he stood up, making his way with Izic on his shoulder, he reached for Elam and found him just as upset as he was about the mess they'd made.

I've been looking for you. You've been blocked from me. Casdon wondered what other magic had been working to get him and Elam to talk to their mothers, and told him where he was now. *I'm walking toward where she is now. I'm nearly to the lake as we speak. Can you meet me there?*

He told Izic what he was going to do, and as soon as the brownie left his shoulder, he let his dragon take him.

Izic said he'd meet him there as well and moved away. Casdon took to the skies just as he heard a shot ring out. He felt the bullet chip some of the stone off the cave as he moved up. Christ, that had been close.

The man below him was cursing. He could see him there, his gun at his side, looking up at him. Casdon might have gone down to deal with him, but he had a feeling should he do that then all would be lost with Ariannona. The need to be with her right now was great. But he did let Asher know what he'd seen.

He shot at you? I mean, he really tried to kill you for a second time? Casdon said that he was pretty mad that he'd missed him too. *Well, we're dealing with him right now. Come here and you can take me to where you saw him.*

I can't. I'm on a mission. He asked him why the hell not and what mission could be more important than this. *I'm going to save Ariannona for us. Elam is on his way there too. We can't let her die, Asher.*

No you can't. And it's about time. Tell me what you find, and for the love of everything, please be careful. This man, this slayer person, is going to have to pay for what he's put us through. Casdon told him he would. *Be careful, and let me know when you're returning. I'll keep an eye out for the three of you.*

~~~

Ralph cursed and stomped his way all the way back to his camper. The fucking gun. A dragon had been all but his when he'd had his gun jam up. He knew that his first shot had gone wild and he'd have to get off a second one quickly. But something messed up and he didn't get his prize.

When it just turned from man to beast, it had been all he could do not to piss himself, but he'd had his gun up to kill whatever he could see when he saw the man standing there. Then just as suddenly as he'd come into view, he'd turned into a great dragon and had disappeared.

A fucking blue dragon. A damn fucking blue dragon was right there, and I missed it. Ralph looked at his home now, ever cautious of simply going inside and assuming that he was safe. Twice now he'd been awakened in the middle of the night by some sound or another. And once while he'd been in his shower, something had bumped against the camper so hard that all his toiletries had fallen to the floor. Just when he bent to pick them up, he'd been hit on the head by something and had gone out like a light. He thought himself very lucky that the water had run out before he'd drowned himself.

The window that he'd broken was now covered in cardboard and tape. He'd thought about going into town, driving the big rig in to get some much needed supplies, as well as the window fixed. But he'd been sleeping poorly and wasn't sure he wanted to chance missing a great opportunity to bag himself a dragon. He had to go soon, however. If it rained, everything was going to get soaked. He'd have to go tomorrow at the latest before he ran out of the most basic of things to eat as well.

After checking out the entire camper, he made his way back to the kitchen. He was down to eating just crackers and water now. Everything that he'd brought seemed to have run out quicker than he thought it should. He wanted to blame it on whatever was haunting him, but he was pretty sure, by the tightness of his clothing, that it was all him. Smiling, he sat at the table to eat.

Whenever he had bouts of depression on how shitty his life had become, he'd think of the money he'd have when he got him a dragon. Right now he had nothing to his name but a great many bills and bad news. Even the once in a great while trips to town to get his mail, from the post office box he'd set up all those months ago, was depressing. But if he'd killed the dragon, the blue one, that would have given him it all.

The noise startled him. Ralph sat there for several seconds, just trying to feel where it was coming from, vibrations from somewhere to tell him if it was inside or out. But when the camper took a sudden hard shake, he held onto the table top like his life depended on it. Then when the howling started, sounding like it was coming from beneath the camper, he went to get his guns, and then he was going to brave the outdoors.

As soon as he stepped his foot out the door and was standing on the ground, the door slammed shut. The lock turning had him dropping his weapon and rushing to see if it had really locked him out. But before he could go a foot, he saw the woman standing in the field.

"Who are you? What are you doing here?" He reached for his gun, which was just far enough away that he had to stretch to get it, and it moved. Not because he'd touched it, but it moved away from him. Toward the woman. And when he looked at her again, she had cut the difference between them in half. "Who are you? What are you doing here? I have a gun."

"You have nothing that I fear."

He backed up when she floated toward him. She'd taken no steps, not flown like the dragon, had but floated, like she had no legs and just used air to get to him. When he backed up against the camper, she was standing about five feet from him. "You're Ralph Desmond Sharp, aren't you? A man who thinks to get him a dragon to sell. You should know that's going to get you into a great deal of trouble."

"What are you talking about?" He knew though, knew just what she was talking about. "Who are you? Why are you here, out here scaring me?"

"Do I scare you, Ralph Desmond Sharp?" The way she said his name, his full name, made him think that she was trying to curse him. And when she put out her hand to touch him, he whimpered as he tried to melt himself into his home. "I should scare you, you fool. Killing dragons is something that is forbidden."

"No one believes them to be alive, so how can I be breaking any law? I'm here on a hunting trip. What I find, if I find anything, is mine. I have permits." She laughed, throwing back her head and laughing like he'd told the greatest joke of all time. "I asked you who you were. I demand that you answer me."

"Demand, is it? And how is it that you feel you have any ability to command one such as myself?" He wasn't sure what she was asking him so said nothing. "You? A mere human thinks to tell me what to do? I think not."

Her manner of speech made him think of those old shows his mamma used to watch, where the women wore long dresses and the men hats and coats to go out and have tea. He couldn't remember what the storyline was about, but he did remember thinking it was the most boring movie. When she laughed again, he watched her.

"The dragon that you helped to kill, Dawod. Do you realize that he was as old as the earth? That his death was one of the most felt deaths of any dragon?" Ralph asked her where the body was. "Gone. His magic is where it should be, too. With the earth faerie. Her babe and their family will use it in ways that you cannot even imagine the riches they will receive by getting such a boon."

"That money is mine." She asked him what money. "The riches, then. The ones that family stole from me, that's all mine. I killed him."

"This is not a thing you should say lightly. To kill one, to brag on the death of one so great, it is forbidden." He rolled his eyes, no longer afraid of the woman or whatever she was. "Besides, I only said riches. I never said money. Is this what you are doing here? Trying to collect on money?"

He was confused. He'd only admit that to himself, but the way she kept bouncing around, twisting up her words and his, was making him pissy. Ralph felt something move over him, sort of touch in his head, and he rubbed his nose, coming away with a little blood. Now he had fear with his anger.

"Hey, bitch, it's what makes the world go around. But no, not just the money. There's the fame that I'll get when they figure out that I got one. Then I'm going to take the body and carve it up for my own personal gain." She tisked at him and he smiled. "What, you don't need money where you come from?"

"Nay, I am dead." He thought he could have gone his whole life without hearing that. "I am here to warn you off. Much as the witch did when you first encountered her."

"Witch? You mean that bitch in white? What the fuck is up with her? She sicced a bear on me." The dead woman laughed and he felt himself getting braver by the second. "You tell her when you see her that she tries that shit again and I'm going to blow a hole through her head."

The woman moved then, so quickly that it was a blur. The distance between them was closed, her body pressed against his so tightly that he was once again nearly one with the walls of his home. And when she licked his cheek, Ralph felt his belly tighten and his balls come so close to his body that he cupped them in his hand to try and ease some of the pressure.

"Do you know what I am?" Her voice was darker now, almost like she'd been strangled. He had no idea why that thought popped into his head, but now all he could think about was being strangled. "Vampire."

He didn't think that his blood moved, stopping his heart in the process. His breath stopped moving in and out of his lungs to the point where he felt as if he were deep in the pits of hell and there was nothing to breathe. When he closed his eyes, trying to convince himself that this was a dream, they were torn open, her fingers pulling them apart to see her. Ralph looked into her eyes, not having any way, it seemed, to look away. And there he saw evil. Pure, unadulterated evil.

"Please, don't hurt me." She laughed, and her body, cold against his, moved without a sound. And when she tilted his neck, he knew that she was going to tear his throat out and leave him there to be drained. "Please. I didn't mean any harm."

"Do not lie to me." He shook his head, both agreeing with her and trying to dislodge her fingers from his face. "You will leave here. Now. Today, and never return. If I hear of you killing another dragon, I will hunt you down and rip out your throat as I feast upon your blood."

"Please. I beg of you. Don't kill me." She told him to agree. "Yes, I agree. I won't return. I won't kill another dragon. I'll leave here today."

The bite to his throat had him cry out in pain. And when she slurped at his wound, noisily sucking his blood from his body, he held onto the wall and begged for his life. She touched his cock, wrapped her hand around him as she drank from him, and Ralph was sickened when he got hard, his body betraying him even as he was being murdered.

Come for me. He shook his head, trying once again to get her away from him. But he was getting harder, his balls filling. And then he was naked, his cock in her bare hands. He looked down at himself as she jerked him, her hand sliding up and down his cock using his own pre juices. *Come for me. Then I'll let you fuck me.*

"No. I don't want to fuck you." The laughter, like the voice, was in his head. And when he came, crying out his release, she pulled her mouth from his throat to his chest. The bite to his nipple felt like she was trying to get to his heart. Yet he was getting hard again, something that never happened to him. As she went to her knees in front of him, Ralph once again begged her to stop.

"Tell me no." She licked his cock from root to tip. "If you say you do not wish to fuck me, and mean it, then I will leave you here, your cock hard and full."

She stood up, her body as naked as he was now, and touched her nipple. He wanted to taste her there. Suckle the tiny morsel in his mouth until he came on her. As her fingers slid down to her pussy, he touched his hardening cock, fisted it so that when she moaned at her own touch, he nearly pulled his cock from his body.

"I want to fuck you."

She nodded, her body already moving around so that she leaned over his picnic table, spread out for him like dinner. Her ass was at his cock, her breasts swinging beneath her. And when he pulled her to him, filled her pussy with his cock, Ralph knew that this was going to be the best fuck of his life. All other thoughts of fear and her being a vampire left his head.

He pounded her hard. And no matter how hard he took her, she would beg him for more. When she stood up, his cock still deep inside of her, he fondled her breasts, tugged on her nipples, and twisted them until she cried out. When she moved away from him, taking her pussy from his cock, he watched her lay on his bed and wondered how that had happened.

"It will be better here, for all of us." He wasn't sure what she meant until he was touched from behind. The hands were large, bigger than his, but they were doing things to his body that he couldn't help enjoying. "He wants to fuck you. While you fuck me."

"Yes." He hadn't thought of sex with another man before. Had even thought it kind of wrong. But the thought of this faceless man fucking him made his cock harder, his need spike. When the woman on the bed, his bed, begged him to come to her, he got on it with her. With her body spread out for him, he moved up between her legs as the bed shifted behind him. The man took his ass in his hands and he had a moment of panic, a moment of fear, but the woman spread her nether lips and he could see her clit swollen with need for him.

"Fuck my cunt." He moved up her, his cock in his hand as the man behind him touched his ass. Then something touched inside of him, a finger he was sure, but it stilled him in movement. "He's going to take you there. Fuck you hard like you're going to do me. And when he comes in your ass, you're going to fill my pussy at the same time."

The moment he slid inside of her, his ass felt as if it were being ripped apart. Screaming against the pain of it, trying his best to get away, he slammed his cock deeper into the woman and she cried out in pleasure.

Ralph didn't move...he didn't have to as the man did all the work. His arms were on either side of him now, his cock sliding in and out of him so quickly and so hard that he knew he was going to die. Then the most incredible thing happened. He felt his balls fill, his cock ache to empty. When the man behind him licked his shoulder, he knew that he was going to be bitten and needed it...wanted to feel him sinking his teeth into him like he needed his next heartbeat. The woman dug her nails into his arms, holding him while she cried out she was coming, and he was bitten. Not by just the man, but by both of them. Ralph came so hard that he saw stars and breasts. Yes, he thought, there were breasts in his vision as he simply slipped away.

Chapter 7

"Mistress?" Ariannona opened her eyes and looked at the tiny figure in front of her. He'd been waking her off and on over the past...well, she had no idea how long it had been going on, but she was too tired to care any longer. Her body was spent. "Mistress? They have come here."

"All right, Izic." She closed her eyes again, not caring what he was talking about. "When you come back the next time, I wish for you to bring me a rose. You know where they are hidden."

"We have them. And we know how to use them." The voice wasn't Izic's. She wasn't even sure whose it was, but she nodded. The rose had been both her blessing and her curse. But it was magical. "Wake enough to take some of the broth, love. We have to help you."

"I've no need of food or broth, Izic. Please, just leave me in peace." The man said no and she looked up at him. "Elam? What kind of trick is this?"

"No tricks. Come on, love. Drink some of this. And I must say, that is the most beautiful rose garden I've ever seen. My mom would have loved it." She tried to sit up, but her body was too weak, her arms not able to hold her up for long. "Casdon has gone to get a net to carry you back to the house with. I wasn't sure that you'd be able to hold onto him while he flew."

"I'm dying." He told her not if he could help it. "What are you doing here? I thought you ill."

"I was. For a little while anyway. But then I had a long talk with my mom and she straightened me out. Here, eat this." The spoon was shoved in her mouth and she had no choice but to swallow or spit it back at him. And that was sounding tempting. "If you spit it out, we're just going to be here longer. Now drink this up so I can get you ready to go."

"I'm not going anywhere with you."

He said nothing but put another spoonful of the rose soup in her mouth. She had to admit, it was delicious, but she was mad at him, or she thought she should have been, and tried to turn her head when he put another spoonful at her lips.

When he said her name, she turned to look at him. Ariannona thought he looked defeated. And for some reason, that hurt her. He watched her, the spoon in his hand, the soup steaming in the other hand, and she wanted to hold him. Then he started to speak.

"I spoke to my long dead mother today. Did you know that was possible?" She said that she'd learned that anything was possible if you wanted it badly enough. "Yes, that's true. But to be honest with you, I really didn't want to speak to her. I wanted to...well, that's beside the point."

"You wished to talk to her because you thought her not able to give you answers you did not want to hear." He smiled at her and said that was it precisely. "What, pray, does that have to do with you being here with me? I thought you done with me. You'd be better off not staying here. You will get ill again."

"No I won't. But I never really started with you, did I? Me nor Casdon. But we're going to work on that. As soon as you're healthy. But back to the conversation with my mom. She didn't really speak to me as much as she made me aware of how angry and.... My father told me he was ashamed of me. I don't think I had ever heard him say that to anyone. And I don't want him to feel that way about me ever again."

"I've no idea what you're talking about. Where is Izic? I asked him not to tell anyone where I was." The brownie cleared his throat, and she looked at him. "You brought them here? You told them what I asked you not to?"

"Nay, mistress, I did not bring them here at all. I might have guided them to this cave, but they only asked me where I was living, not about you. And I told no living soul about your being ill, just as I promised. Nor did I mention to a living soul that you were dying here. Alone in this cave." She eyed him, and he smiled at her. "I did tell the lady Sally and the queen. The original one, not the one that lives in the big house. I needed to unburden myself, as it were. The promise and the result of it made me sad, and I needed to speak with someone or be sadder still."

She felt betrayed. And when Elam asked her to take another bite, she turned her head from him and stared down the long tunnel that led deep into the mountain. It was where she should have gone when Izic left her the first time. He was terrified of the darkness. Then none of this would be happening.

"You should not be here. You will get ill again, as I said." He said he wouldn't, not now. "And why is that? Have you a sudden trust of me?"

"Yes." She looked at him, trying to gauge if he was lying to her. "I've been wrong before, but never had I hurt someone that I love so much by it. I am and will be forever sorry for not trusting you. I'd like to tell you that it'll never happen again, that I'll never make you so mad at me that you wish to run. But I promise you now that I never meant to harm you in any way."

"You do not trust me even now." He nodded, then shook his head. "You do that a great deal. Are you so indecisive that you cannot come up with an answer?"

"No. I'm trying to tell you that I trust you. With every fiber of my being." He put the bowl down, and she was surprised to see that his hands were blue. She asked him about it. "I made your broth while Casdon found the mushrooms that went with it. I had no idea that there was a garden so close to the lakes, and Izic said that it was all your making. But the rose petals had to be fresh, and since I had no idea if you meant your handful needed to be crushed or any handful, I sort of picked too many. But they've gone to good use. I plan to put the others on my mom's grave. She'll love that."

She looked over at her friend and wondered what other things he might have told them. She wondered aloud how long she'd been there. Elam told her only a few hours. And a day.

"You've been here for an entire day and a part? For what reason?" He told her because he loved her. "You might, but you have to have them both for you to keep from getting ill again. It's not worth the effort you have wasted here today."

"I think it is." He leaned back on the stone he was on and watched her as he continued. "You are very beautiful. I never told you that before. But Christ, woman, you are the most beautiful woman I've ever seen."

"Nay. You aren't to tell me untruths." She shook herself mentally. "You take me to the past with your flattery. I have worked hard in not sounding as if I've come from another century."

"But you have and I love it." Ariannona wanted him gone, but before she could tell him again this was a mistake, the room darkened for a moment when someone walked into the mouth of the cave. "Ah, here he is. Casdon. Look, she wakes. I think her still weak, but we shouldn't have any trouble getting her home."

Just as she was ready to tell them both to go to hell, the dragon shifted to man and came to her. When he kissed her, pulling her body to his, all she could think about was how much she loved these men and the feelings that they'd awakened in her. When he stepped back she was flustered and felt out of sorts, and wanted to snap at them both.

"I should like to make love to you, right here, right now." Her body heated and she looked around for Izic. "I sent him on his way. He's to prepare the room at our house so that you will be comfortable. You will be…we're going to make sure of it."

"We're in a cave. You must be mad. There isn't any bed soft enough, and the ground is cold and hard." Elam stood up and started pulling his shirt off. "I've been here for two days. I'm not fit for making love. And you might get ill again."

"We're not going to be sick again. I've told you that." She looked at Casdon, who was naked, stroking his cock. Elam laughed a little as he continued. "See, he is as ready for you as I am. Let us come on your lovely body. Then when we get you home, we'll take a nice long hot shower together and then you'll be clean. So we can muss you again."

"I don't want this." Her body was telling them a different story; she knew that they could smell her heat. "Don't do this, Elam. Casdon, please. You have to see reason."

"The only reason I can see where this does not happen is that you tell us no. Do you want us to stop?" Elam was naked now too, his cock so thick and long that her mouth watered to take him inside of her. She didn't even care which way he took her. As his hand moved up and down his cock his eyes closed, and he moaned as he continued. "The thought of coming on you. Marking you with my cum."

"I want to suck you. Feel you fucking my mouth as you have before." He nodded and took a step toward her as she got to her knees. Running her hands down her body to make her clothing disappear, she felt hands on her skin as she exposed herself to her men. Casdon wasted no time in going behind her, and lifted her up so that she was impaled on his cock. "Elam, come to me."

He moved to her, his cock still in his hand, and she took him in her mouth. The cock at her back made her needy and wetter, and when Casdon slid his fingers onto her clit, she rode him with the same vigor she used to fuck Elam with her mouth.

"Christ yes, love. That's it. Take me, make me come." She was going to come...Casdon was holding her pussy with one hand while her breasts and nipples were being abused by the other. She was on fire...everywhere she was touched, even at the back of her throat, she felt it in her heart. They loved her.

"I need to shift places." Before she could think what Casdon was saying to her, she was on her feet and being kissed by Elam. His hands, like Casdon's, were massaging her, branding her like she wanted. And when Casdon said her name, she looked down at him lying on the ground.

He had turned so that his feet were out, his head now resting on his arms. When he fisted his cock again and told her to come cover him, she moved to lower herself over his cock with Elam's help. When she was there, her pussy filled with him, Elam stood in front of her and she took him in her mouth again.

Riding him. That's what she was doing, riding Casdon. His hands now held her hips as his own body moved up and into hers. When she felt Elam curl his hand to the back of her head, she cupped his balls, felt the lovely weight of them while he slid his cock down past the tightness of her throat. And then he filled her, his cum burning as it slid past the muscles there. It gave her such a wondrous feeling. But she needed more. Had to have all of them.

His cock touched off another powerful climax. She cried out even as Elam pounded her throat and Casdon her pussy. When Elam pulled from her mouth, cum still spraying from his tip, she was rolled to her back and Casdon fucked her hard.

Elam watched them, his cock hard as it had been in her mouth, her saliva and his cum making his stroking himself smooth. And when he leaned back, holding his balls for her to see him, she wrapped her legs around Casdon's hips and held him tightly to her as she watched her other true love masturbate.

It was like being a part of everything. She could feel Elam's hand on his cock as if she were stroking him. Casdon's balls felt like they were giving her pussy a hard and firm punch each time he filled her. And when he cried out, Casdon telling her that he was coming, she felt herself roll with him, her body taking pleasure as much as she was giving it.

The first spray of his cum shooting up from his cock had her screaming out her second release. Casdon fucked her harder, his body seemingly becoming a part of hers. He cried out again, and she did as well, screaming out their names as her body came apart. She slipped away, knowing that no matter what, they'd care for her.

~~~

Ralph woke in his bed. He lay there for several minutes, letting the things that he'd done, the things that had been done to him, wash over him. Reaching out slowly with just his fingers, almost too afraid to check, he made sure he was alone in his bed before he opened his eyes.

There wasn't anyone with him, thankfully, and when he rolled to his back, looking up at the ceiling, he realized that he wasn't sore. His body felt fine. Sitting up in his bed, he checked his body for bite marks. Tiny holes at his throat and nipples where he knew that he'd been bitten. Nothing.

Getting up, stretching his long body, he felt...well, he felt wonderful. Like he'd slept for a full night, his body relaxed and fit. Searching his arms over his head in the bathroom while looking in the mirror, he not only didn't see anything out of the ordinary, but he was also surprised to find that he had no bruising and no cuts. Ralph knew that at one point the man had cut him with his long claw-like nails and had drank from him. The woman had beaten him with a whip, and his body had been bloodied and sore.

The bed was pristine too, and his body unharmed. Ralph was beginning to think it had been a dream. A very vivid but bad dream. He moved to take a shower, turning on the water and looking at the mirror over the sink. As he brushed his teeth, he thought of all the things he had to do today. Going into town had to be a priority.

Scrubbing up, he started to whistle and then sing. He'd done that a lot before he'd married, singing in the shower at the top of his lungs. His ex-wife had hated it, telling him that he had no voice and that he made her head pound when he belted out such a monstrosity so early in the morning. He sang louder today, uncaring of the notes he didn't hit or the words he probably did not get right. When he got out, drying his body all over, he moved to his bedroom again and began pulling on clothes.

Going into the kitchen, he pulled down a bowl and a box of cereal to eat. He was making a mental list of things he had to do when he looked out the window over the sink. As he stood there, the implications of what he was seeing registering in his mind, the bowl and its contents dropped to the floor and shattered into a huge mess.

"No. No. No." He sat down, not on the chair as he'd been aiming for, but in the cereal and broken pottery that was on the floor. The longer he sat there, the harder his mind worked. There was no way he was seeing what he was seeing. And if he was, then he'd done it. Latching onto that thought, he reasoned through each thing he was seeing.

The window was fixed. The glass that he'd sort of half-assed cleaned up was gone. The dirty dishes were done, stacked neatly on the counter. Even the cereal he'd nearly eaten hadn't been there before. It was as if he'd had a cleaning crew come in and clean up after him.

"I took it to town last night. Got it fixed, and I...and I did some shopping too." That would explain away the now fixed window, he thought, and the food all lined up in a neat row on the counter. Bags neatly folded, the receipt right there where he could see it. "Yes. I traveled all night and that's why I'm so fit this morning. I ate in town and came back exhausted and slept well."

He kept telling himself that was what he'd done. Traveled and got things fixed. Grocery shopped and filled his cabinets. The water he'd used for his shower would have also been refilled. And he'd bet his sewage tanks were not just emptied, but clean as well. It was what he would do, make sure he was ready for a long stay. He'd hated going to the lake and carting water up from it to fill his empty water tanks.

Standing up, he wasn't surprised to see that he'd cut himself. A long open wound on his leg bled while he gathered his kit and cleaned it up.

He continued to find things. Things that he'd left undone in favor of the dragon hunting. Small things and large tasks too. The laundry was done, pressed, and put in the drawers. The pull-out sofa that he'd been using as a bed was now a seat again, the pillows on it fluffed up and in each corner. He put a bandage on his wound and nodded to himself. Yes, he'd been very busy, it seemed.

"I was just exhausted, that's all. It's why I have little to no memory of the events. I did all this so that I could hunt all day. Spend my time finding the dragon I saw yesterday." It bothered him slightly that he was talking to himself. Not only asking questions, but answering them as well. He decided that while it might seem insane to most, he was quite happy with the conversations that he was having. No one would give him the answers he wanted but himself, he thought with a grin.

Instead of going out, however, he elected to stay at the camp site. There were things he needed to do anyway, he reasoned, and what better time to get on them than when he was fully rested. The windows needed washing. The carpets swept up. All things he knew had to be done, and today was as good a day as any.

Ralph was on the top of his camper, sweeping off the debris and leaves, when he saw a movement. Lying down, not making a sound, he watched the man walk up to his temporary home and knock on the door.

He had no idea who he was. His size made Ralph think of body builders, ones that got on programs and won awards. Even his hands were large, like he could hold a basketball with it and not have any strains on his fingers. Ralph lay there watching the man, as still as one of the trees in the yard surrounding him.

"I only came to talk to you. My name is Asher, Asher Benson." Asher neither looked up nor stepped back from the door when he spoke. "I own the land over there, my brothers and I. I wish to ask you if you know anything of a man who shot at one of my sisters-in-law the other day. And my brother."

Ralph said nothing, but his mind was working. Brother? He'd shot at his brother? And what woman did he speak of? The only one that he'd taken aim at was the woman in white, the one that he'd seen long ago. Then he thought of his dream last night. The woman and the man. He skirted around the memories of them again, as he'd been doing all morning, and listened to Asher when he spoke again.

"There is a rumor that there is a dragon slayer about. One that cowardly hides behind his guns and shoots at mythical creatures." They weren't mythical at all. He'd seen one. But the man spoke as if it were a joke. As if no one believed in dragons. "He's going to hurt someone, this man, if he continues to shoot at innocent people he thinks are dragons."

"They're as real as you." The man looked up at him, and Ralph remembered then that he was supposed to be hiding from him. As he made his way down the ladder, the man moved to where he was going to alight and waited for him. "I've seen them. A blue one the other day in the caves beyond."

"The caves up there?" He pointed in the wrong direction, and Ralph corrected him. He could have kicked himself, because he'd just given himself away. For all he knew this man was a hunter too. Ralph had just given him his trade secret. "Those caves belong to my land. You are trespassing on private property. Did you know that?"

"I only shot in that direction. I wasn't on the land." He felt good about his reasoning until the man grabbed him by the neck and lifted him up as if he weighed no more than a twig. "What are you doing? Put me down."

"You shot at my brother, you idiot. What is wrong with you that you can't tell the difference between a man and a dragon? A creature that does not exist?" Ralph felt his head tighten from lack of air and struggled harder. But he was getting weaker, even as the man shook him hard then tossed him to the ground. "You come near my land and my family again and I will come back here and show you what real wrath feels like when I tear you apart."

"I know what I saw. And I saw a dragon. A great blue one. There was a man there at first. He talked to someone behind him or something. But he was a man. Then he shook himself and turned into this dragon." The man in front of him growled. "I tell you the truth. If that was your brother, then you should check him out. The fucker is a dragon."

The sky darkened overhead. When the man didn't look to see whatever it was, Ralph looked up. And when he fell on his back, the sight he was seeing making him giddy, he looked at the man to tell him to see it too. But he was gone, not a trace of him as Ralph stood up again to see.

As he rounded the corner of the camper, thinking of the direction that the dragons had taken, the man was standing there with three other men, each of them the same size as the one he'd talked to at first.

"You here to hurt me?" The man to Asher's right laughed. "What is it? I've done nothing wrong. I know what I saw."

"So you say. And what is it you saw? Dragons? What do you think people are going to say to you when you tell them you saw dragons?" The other man looked up, then back at him. "There are no such things as dragons."

"I know what I saw." Asher looked at the two men with him, then back at him. There was a hardness about him now, like he was done being nice. If he ever was. Ralph took a step back when Asher crossed his arms over his massive chest and glared at him.

"You come near our land, or shoot in the direction of it, then I will come back here. Do you hear me?" Ralph nodded and said he'd be more careful. "You'd be better off giving up on this folly of yours. It's only going to get you killed."

"So *you* say." Ralph watched the three of them, wondering what sort of steroids they took to be that big. He thought their muscles had muscles, and he was slightly jealous of them. When the third man laughed again, Ralph asked him what he thought was so funny.

"The vampire that you slept with last night, she left you a note." Ralph backed up so quickly when the man reached for him that he nearly fell on his ass. "I have no plans of touching you. I'm only reaching for the paper. I wasn't going to hurt you. Yet."

It was the *yet* that terrified him. The threat of it had his balls tightening again. When he handed him the note, the pretty lavender paper with a scent on it that made his dick harden, Ralph held it in his hand and saw it shake slightly.

"She's not real. It was...the two of them, it was a dream." Asher said it didn't appear to be to him, not since he was holding proof of it in his hand. "No, you don't understand. I was fit today. I'd slept so well and I feel so good. There was work to be done here, things that I'd been putting off. I had the window fixed on my own. Drove into town last night and had it repaired while I had a nice meal and did some shopping."

"No, you didn't. You didn't move this thing. Nothing has moved in months." Even as the man pointed to the lack of tire marks, Ralph was shaking his head. "You haven't left here since you parked it, I think. And you did have a vampire bite you. And the male, he's not a vampire, but her watcher I guess. You've been fucked. If I were you, I'd take some precautions that it doesn't happen again."

"How? How do I keep her from coming to me again? They just appeared in my house here. And then when we started it, this sex, I was suddenly naked and in my bed." None of them said anything, and he felt like he wanted to cry. "I don't know what to do."

No one seemed to have an answer to that either. He noticed that not a one of them would look him in the eye after his confession. It hurt him. Even though he didn't know these men until today, it hurt him to think that they were ashamed of his actions too. Asher was the only one that talked to him just before they left.

"She's an old one, this vampire lover of yours, and when she comes back I don't think she's going to be too happy that you were with us." Ralph had asked him why. "Because we smell like faerie. And witch. And everyone knows that vamps don't get along well with either of those."

Long after they left him standing there, holding the letter like he was afraid it was going to soil him somehow, he thought of the man's final words to him. Ralph had to do something or he was going to be killed. He knew it.

Chapter 8

Gideon loved to work with his sisters. Both of them, even large into their breeding, were keeping up with their studies, and he thought perhaps one of them, if not both, were going to need someone with a great deal more experience than he had very soon now. As a dragon, he'd not been able to play with the kind of magic that they had, but he knew how to move and to fall. He looked up when he saw Ariannona come out of the house across from them. She looked better, pale still, but better than she did when they'd brought her home yesterday.

"Come work with us." Gideon looked at Lindsey when she invited the other woman to come into the yard. "I think we've worn poor Gideon out. Besides, maybe you can show us some things that he can't."

"He's doing well." Gideon bowed to her when she came onto the field with them. He smiled at her when she stood in front of him. "You're holding back. Because of the children?"

"No. I'm holding back because of them." He nodded to his left, and Ariannona turned to look at his brothers. "I fear them more than I do getting these women a bump on the bottom or two."

"I see. But you know that the earth can help them with that as well, don't you?" He shook his head, not understanding. "Watch. You can do this too, all of you can. Nothing will harm them here, not if they're on solid ground. It's part of what the land gives you. Mostly them, but all of you."

Ariannona charged Essie. He tensed, waiting for one or all of the men beside him to attack her, but when she hit Essie, her feet sailing through the air like she was part kite, Essie fell back but never hit the ground.

No one moved as Essie put her feet down and stood. Ariannona stayed where she'd landed, her body hard with whatever came next. Asher came to her, and Gideon was sure she was going to hear about it, but all he did was put out his hand to help her stand. Essie and Lindsey both laughed.

"How did you do that?" Essie hugged Ariannona twice before she continued with her questions. "How did you keep me from falling?"

"I didn't. You're part of the world around you. And it knows everything about you, what you're doing here. What you're doing for not just the earth and the creatures in it, but the world around it. The dragons especially. It is, rightly, keeping you safe. Even from your own folly." Ariannona looked at him. "Should someone charge you, as I did with them, you'd not fall either. The land protects what it considers her own. And with you being a dragon of the lineage that you are, it will protect your kind above all others, save the women."

Almost as if she had summoned them, a swarm of dragons came from the tree line, and it might have been scary if they had all not been about the size of his hand. Gideon and his brothers, all of them, circled the women. Something could have startled them into rushing them, and they were going to be prepared.

The little dragons moved between them to get to the women. Ariannona stood beside him, her body seemingly relaxed, yet ready. When Elam came to them, just leaving the house, he too looked like he had just been woken from his slumber and had not a care in the world. Whatever had bothered the dragons didn't seem to worry anyone but him. Gideon wondered at that when he heard Lindsey laughing behind him.

"They found us." He could see that now. They were all over Lindsey and Essie. Lindsey laughed again. "They said that it wasn't until the witch told them where to go that they knew they'd be safe." Everyone looked at Ariannona.

"That would be Izic, not me. He has been putting the word out that there is a safe haven for them. I had hoped that more and more of them would come because of the slayer." Ariannona nodded toward the dragons. "They're fully grown, and the last of their kind. Several decades ago someone came into the field where they lived and clear-cut the trees, leaving them not just without a place to live and to survive, but it also took out large groups of their families. Izic knew that they'd been struggling to live, so I had him to go find them. It's harder than you think to find a swarm of dragons."

Gideon didn't understand why they didn't just go and hunt him down, this slayer of dragons. There were enough places around here to hunt and to feed yourself. Why his family? Why the dragons that meant no one any harm?

People apparently had been hunting them for years—centuries really—and he knew that. It didn't make it any better, and he didn't understand why anyone would want to kill dragons.

Gain. Fame. You name it, there have been people looking to kill dragons for as long as we've been on this earth. He looked over at Onimia when he spoke through their link. *There have been slayers, many of them since before my parents were born. And I think there will be some even after this man leaves this earth.*

Why not go out, find him, and burn him to a crispy fritter? You know, ash is hard to do testing on. Or we could find a nice deep hole to put him in. Drive that stupid noisy thing of his over the cliff and...no, that won't work. Pollution and all. We could sell it? I like that idea much better. Why not go all out, kill him, and make a profit too? Onimia was staring at him now, and he had to hold back a laugh. There was a small green dragon hanging on his ear lobe at the moment. *I tell you what, you go to the skies, find him, and I'll tie him up and you can take him out.*

Because, you dolt, we are no better than them if we do that. Gideon hurt, he was trying so hard not to laugh now. The dragon was looking like he was making a home for himself on Onimia's head by moving his hair around to suit some idea he had of furniture. *How would that look it if someone came here looking for this man...his wife, children? Do you think they'd be happy to know that we killed him?*

No, but it's also not all right that he kills our own. And you heard what Ariannona said the other day...his family has been slayers for centuries. Perhaps if we took care of the problem now, we'd not have to worry about it in the future. Onimia only huffed at him.

To be honest, he was just joking. Not about taking care of the man—no, not that—but about burying his body in the mountains. Not that he'd do that either. He was just tired, that was it. Tired of it all.

There was so much tension of late that he was beginning to feel like they would never be able to be happy. Gideon looked over at Lindsey as she rubbed her belly. It was a sight to behold, he thought, to see someone that you loved swollen with a child. There was a true sign that something good could come from the worst kind of evil shit.

Cleaning up, making sure the dragons were well, it was time to get back to work.

As he made his way to the castle with the rest of them, he thought of what they were doing, and why. It was going to be grand, he thought, to have it the way it had been. Not just the castle itself, but the land around it as well. Recently trees had been planted and a kitchen garden had been placed; herbs were sprouting up even now.

Even some of the decorations added to the ancient feel of the place…a fountain that they'd gotten, and a row of fencing that was made of steel and stone. There was even a little garden that had a few gnomes in it, just for fun. Not many, but a few of them were being put aside to fill in the spaces around the keep as soon as it was finished. He looked at Akassa, Simeon's dragon, when he pulled a great stone from the fallen ones.

"We need a party." He'd not meant to say it aloud, but now that he had, he could see that it had merit. "Not on the scale we could have when the castle is ready, but something fun. We've been working so hard." Asher asked him what sort of party. Before he could think of what he meant, Shane spoke.

"Pizza or burgers on the grill. Potato salad like Mom used to make. I know that it's a bit early for it, but cucumber and tomato salad too. And fresh slices of tomatoes and lettuce still warm from the sun." Everyone stopped working and was staring at Shane as he continued. "Burgers...not steaks, just plain burgers. Cheese that Elbert makes...you know, the peppery kind that is hot enough to make you drink a gallon of tea, but so good you just can't stop eating it."

"And remember that coconut cake that Mom would make for us? The one that she told us she slaved over for days, and we all knew that it only took the same time as a regular cake?" Keion laughed. "I loved her cakes. We had them so seldom, but man were they good."

"She did that so you'd appreciate them more. Supply and demand, she called it." His dad, who had been planting saplings with Essie, joined them. "And her corn cakes. Oh my, it's been so long since I tasted her corn cakes. She'd get them just right, the crisp on the edges that I loved. And butter. Oh, how I miss that butter she made."

"You should do it." Gideon looked at Ariannona when she spoke. "I mean, the dragons, they would love to help you with that. The new ones, they have been working with humans without their knowledge for a long time. Instead of stealing from them—you know, bits of blankets, scraps of food—they'd do things in return for the items that they'd need. I know that a few of them that arrived today have been working in a dairy for years."

"Oh, I love that idea. You think they could help with the churning? Butter in them little papers, it just ain't the same as a crock of homemade butter." His dad rubbed his hands together, and Gideon thought of all the times their dad had done that when he had a plan. "We should do it. Been a long time since we just had us a little party for no reason. I'm thinking that Elbert can whip up some of those things for us. And then there is the picnic tables. We have to have picnic tables to eat under the trees."

Asher began moving stone, then the rest of them followed. But the planning never stopped. Assignments were made to each person. Ariannona was going to ask the dragons what they could do. Keion was to find one of the bigger dragons and ask him to help fell a couple of trees for tables. They'd make them sturdy so they could use them for years. Even as he was sweating, feeling the heat of the day and the strain on his back, Gideon felt better for it.

"You did a good thing." He looked at Asher and asked him what he meant. "Getting us thinking about something else besides slayers and death. There has been a great deal of that lately."

"I was really just being selfish, Asher. I really did want to have some fun." Asher said that was fine too, that he'd shared his need with the rest of them, and it was apparent that they all had been thinking the same thing. "Thank you. For everything."

"Nay, Gideon, thank you. You're a good brother and my friend as well. There are few families that can say that about each other and mean it." Gideon nodded and bent to pick up one of the stones. As soon as it was free of the dirt, he looked down at where it had been.

~~~

Elam wanted to go to the barn and bring back the backhoe that had been delivered only a few days ago. Of course when the truck had arrived to bring it to them, he'd thought it was something different. Grown trees, the invoice had said. Even a fool could see that they had no such use for grown trees, living where they did. But when it was unloaded, the magic hiding it from the world, the men left, telling them if they had any trouble with the trees getting ill to call them and they'd come out. Sure, we'll do that, Asher had told them.

"Be careful. You've not an idea what might be under that." His dad, like the rest of them, was excited. This was a find that they'd not expected to see, not this close to the top of the grounds.

Elam had moved back from the sight when it was apparent that there were just too many of them digging around the jewel that had been sticking up from the ground. Then when they saw that it was attached to something, the digging became a lot gentler, the big shovels thrown aside for smaller ones and hands.

"Holy shit, it's a crown." The reverence in Casdon's voice had him looking at the large hole that they'd been able to dig around it. Yes, it was a crown. A large one at that. He wondered if it was Casdon's father's or mother's. "Look at it. Do you think that...? Do you think we're going to find...?"

His father. That was what he'd been trying hard not to say. His father was here, his body under this wreckage since before any of them had been born. To find him, to find the dragon king, was going to be hard on all of them.

"They can help." Everyone turned when Ariannona spoke quietly. "The dragons, they can help. They want to help. Several of them, they knew your father, and they can help where you can't."

"How? What can they do?" Asher wasn't being a dick, he sounded genuinely curious. "I was going to have Essie move the earth, but to be honest, I'm afraid to do that. We really have no idea what we have here."

After Ariannona spoke quietly to Izic, he took off. When he returned after a few minutes, ten little dragons were with him, and most of them sat on the earth close to where the crown had been found. One dragon that had landed on Ariannona's shoulder nodded to Izic. They would do it. Ariannona spoke to Asher and the rest of them.

"This is Drumple. He's what you might call their leader. King, I guess." Asher nodded as the small green dragon left her shoulder and landed on the dirt in front of them. "He said that it would be his honor to help you. But he asks that he might speak to you first."

"Yes. Where does he want to talk to me?" Ariannona shook her head at Asher and smiled. "Why am I getting the feeling that this is more on a personal level than I want to know?"

"Nay, not personal, not really. He knows that you're his king. He also knows that for many years he did the equivalent of your job for his people. Keeping them safe, together, and blessing marriages. All things, he knows, that you would do. He wishes only to speak to you, as in just having a conversation." Asher asked her if he thought himself in trouble. "More than that, Asher; he thinks you might wish to kill him. So he would like to speak to you, talk to you before you end his life, so that he can go to his other world as a happy dragon having spoken to a great king again."

Asher looked at the small dragon, and Elam went to his knees when the others did. His brother was a great man, a better leader than anyone he'd ever known. But this was a task that Elam would be at a lost to deal with. He knew as well as any of them did that Drumple was right. Asher did have every right to kill him.

"You have been a good dragon, Drumple?" The dragon nodded and bowed before him. "I wish you to answer me please. I should like to hear what you have to say for yourself."

"There was a need, sire, a need to keep the order, and I filled it. I am...I was the oldest of us. At nine hundred and some years, I was turned to when times were bad." He bowed again, his head touching the dirt. But this time he didn't rise up. "I knew not that a king had been born. My only thought was to help my family and the families of my friends."

"Thank you." Drumple looked up, then put his head back down when Asher thanked him. "Come on, stand. I wish to honor you for your hard work. Without you taking charge, all would have been lost. You did me a great favor by doing what you did. It is my understanding that you and yours, you're the last of your kind. I must thank you for keeping your family safe so that we might live and grow together here."

"You're not mad at me?" Drumple stood up, his chest puffed out like he had a great pride now. "They told me you'd be the one. A great king like King Anthony was. A good man he was. The best we dragons had ever seen. He was kind to humans too. Kept them fed, well clothed, and assisted them in things that were not of his station. And his lady wife, she'd put out sweets for us daily. Planted them roses too, so we'd have a nice scent in our homes."

"You lived here? In the castle?" Drumple turned to Elam, nodding. "And you know what this is, this crown that we've found? Can you tell us who it belonged to?"

"Oh, aye, sir. We all know. 'Tis the king's." Elam looked at the crown with a new respect. To know for sure that it had sat upon the head of the dragon king, King Anthony, all those millennia ago made the find all the more special. "Would you like for us to bring it up, my lord? We can get into places that you cannot with your hands. We'd be as gentle with him as he was with us. Firm, but getting the job done."

"Yes. Please." Asher stood and the rest of them did as well. "Just be careful not to be harmed in this. We have no idea what might be under it, or even what traps might have been cast upon it."

"We'll be careful, and we'll make sure that if we find more, we'll let you know." The body. They were talking about the body of the king. Would he have had it on during the siege? For some reason Elam didn't think so, but backed up when the other dragons came to the hole.

There were perhaps a hundred of them, along with brownies and faeries. Everyone, it seemed, wanted to be a part of this, to bring...as he'd begun to think of it...bring the king home. Elam looked around. They all felt it, the need to finish this.

As the dragons worked together, getting as much dirt and debris as possible from around the crown, the rest of them worked on the walls. New stone was being cut by their dragons. Each piece of it was being left where it lay for the time being. The other stones, the ones too small to be used, were being set in piles by size, to be used where they could when the need arose. Elam looked around as Ariannona handed him a bottle of water.

"You've done much." He nodded and pulled her in for a quick kiss. "The lower levels, do you know how you're going to go about getting them together?"

"I'm not sure. Asher said something about having Essie and Lindsey go in and see if they can get the earth to move things. We're guessing that is how they did it in the first place. Asked the earth to help." She nodded. "Maybe you could lend them a hand when it comes time for it to happen."

"I can do that. And they did work with the earth. On all of this area." Elam sometimes forgot that she had known the king and queen as well. "When the earth moved to make the rooms below, many people thought the earth was turning inside out. Humans even then understood nothing of the people that they served. Of course, anyone with any magic would have been drained a little. Borrowing from the earth as they'd done made us all a little dizzy."

"It would have been hard work, I imagine, living and working here. And dark too." She shook her head and told him how the light had shone up from the bottom. "You mean there is an outside entrance to the lower levels? Is it around here?"

"Yes. Beyond there, the big mountain. It would have been the way that they brought in the servants and food." He asked her to take him there. Asher came with them, as did Casdon as his dragon, as they walked to the place she'd remembered. "I know that there were great stones put in place. And then wooden ones used to reinforce on the inner walls of it in the event of an attack from this area. I don't think that anyone but the help knew about it. I did, of course. A woman I stayed with at times was cook in the kitchens that weren't a part of the castle."

"The bakery." She nodded at his statement. "We have the layout of the castle, and someone had written that there were other buildings to be put in. A drying room, a looming room, as well as a smoke house for meats. But if there were a few off-site buildings, we can't seem to locate any of them. And the plans don't talk about them being finished either."

"Because they were never meant to be a part of the whole. The king wanted to keep his people safe from all that might come to harm them. I don't think he expected to be attacked through his own front door. Or perhaps he did. I'm not sure." Just as they rounded the side of the mountain that the castle was a part of, the buildings, now overgrown with trees, came into view. "These buildings were not a part of the castle — not attached, I mean — because the king didn't want the people working in them to know the workings of the castle. They came and went as they needed. And by the same route, the people working the castle keep would not know where the entrance was either. Guards would bring in the food stuffs, and only them. It was his way of keeping everyone safe."

"Elbert never mentioned it either." Ariannona said he might not have been aware of it, as he was working inside the building rather than out. "But how did they think the food came in and out of the castle? Magic?"

"Perhaps. Most of them would have been aware on some level that they worked for and served dragons. They would see them in the skies and know that they were there. But as for the magical part of it, even with the dragons about, they didn't want to think of what they were, I think. Even back during that time, witches for the most part were burned alive. Only the very strong, as well as the ones that the king and queen used, would have been left to their own business."

They made their way down a path that was worn but starting to become part of the forest that held it again. Trees that he was sure had not been there when the path was being used by the people working here were now as big as he was. Stones too, large ones, and he was sure pieces of the castle were in the pathway now. When they ended up where he thought the back of the castle would be, he looked at the large stone walls and then at her.

"You cannot see it." He looked again, as did Asher and Casdon. "It's because you were not supposed to. Come, I'll show you what only a very few knew about the stone walls on this side of the entrance. I think...perhaps I've been wrong all along, but I thought I got this information from the king by accident. Like maybe a lot of stuff I got from him, which seemed random and useless, was what he really meant for me to have."

She moved to the walls and touched her fingers to a seemingly narrow crack in it. There were several, he noticed, but she followed one, kept to the path like she knew what she was about. As soon as she ran her fingers down the length of it, he could see a bright light shining from where she'd been. When she stepped back after touching a few of the holes that had formed, they all did as well. And when the stone moved, knocking trees out of its way, smaller stones as well, Elam knew why Anthony had done it.

"If they did not know the path to take nor had any magic, then it would have only looked like a stone that had been injured." Ariannona nodded. "Do you suppose it's safe to go in?"

"Yes. I think we have to enter. But we'll wait for more daylight. And the rest of the family. This is something that we'll all need to be a part of." Asher looked at Ariannona and smiled. "You will have to teach this to us. This pattern. It's not as easy as you made it look, I think."

"No, it's not. I did not show it all to you because...well, I wasn't sure you'd want everyone to know it. I think it smart that you do, but I would, if I were you, limit this knowledge to just your family. When you get the castle up and going, it would do you well to have a point of escape."

Escape. Yes, they'd need that, Elam thought. If for no other reason than safety. One or two of those reasons might involve them being under attack, but he didn't think that was any more likely than one of them getting swallowed up by the earth. It could happen, he supposed, but the likelihood of it was low.

"Good thinking. Yes, I like that idea." Asher asked her to show the three of them how to close then open the door several times. It really wasn't that easy to follow. What they'd not seen was that her other hand was following another pattern, and you had to keep them both straight as it was unlocked. "How many mistakes can you make before it doesn't allow you to enter?"

When she didn't answer him, Asher turned to Ariannona. She had the most peculiar look on her face, and Elam might have thought it funny if he wasn't nervous about her answer. When she looked at the wall then back at Asher, Elam knew this was going to be great.

"I'm pretty sure that it knows you're the king." Asher nodded but still looked confused. "Command it, Asher. Give it a command and I'm pretty sure that it will heed you."

Asher looked at the wall. He looked...well, Elam thought he looked terrified. And when he backed from it, his hands behind his back, Elma asked him what was wrong.

"I'm not sure, but the thought that I can command a stone to move for me gives me the willies. I think perhaps we'll table that task for a later date." He looked visibly shaken by the idea. "So for now, we'll just use the pattern. All right?"

The other buildings were looked at, but none of them wanted to go inside the buildings, nor did they seem inclined to even venture too close. It wasn't as if they were afraid, Elam thought, but sort of overwhelmed by it all. He knew that he was a little. There was so much to learn about this place, the people that worked here, even the things that they'd done to keep their lives, for the most part, simple and safe. Elam wondered if, when they finished the castle and all of the surrounding buildings, they'd use some of the old ways or keep it as modern as they could. He was all for a mixture of both, really.

They made their way back to the keep, and Ariannona said she'd have Izic check out the other buildings for them. She knew that one of them would have been a drying house, and thought perhaps there might be some things still there that they could use.

As soon as they were at the keep again, Elam knew that something had happened. And whatever it might have been was where the dragons had been working. He was almost afraid to go and see.

Chapter 9

Ralph caught himself several times over the next couple of days simply staring off into the woods. There wasn't anyone there, and he'd not heard anything that he knew of to make him just stand still and look, but he still found himself doing it. And the slightest sound or movement in the camper had him screaming like a kid and running for cover.

His mind wandered to the note again. It was simple in its message, but no less scary. "See ya." That was all it said, just those two words. And for some odd reason, it made him all jumpy and out of sorts.

He'd been outside of the camper for most of the morning. Twice he'd had to go to the bathroom, and had simply pissed on a tree. He was afraid of the place. Not the camper so much as being caught inside it. Ralph was going over the edge and he knew it.

To call his mobile home a camper was really downgrading what it was. It had so much more in it than his house had had, and it was all new and modern as well.

The bedroom had a king-sized bed with a dresser big enough to hold all his clothing. Even a closet if he put his mind to hanging things up in it. The big screen television was hooked up to satellite that was coming from the dish on the top. He had his own bathroom. There was a second bedroom as well, with a set of bunkbeds that held one twin and one double sized mattress. Two built in dressers as well as a television were in there, and a game system that hadn't been out of the box yet. The living room boasted two large recliners, a love seat, and an entertainment center that housed not just a fine stereo system, but another big screen television and game system that he had opened and had enjoyed on rainy days. The hardwood floors were beautiful, and it had several windows he could open if he didn't want to use his air conditioning.

The kitchen was state of the art, with a microwave unit, oven, and stove top. There was lots of cabinet space too, as well as counter tops. He had a coffee maker, blender, and anything else he might want to use stashed over the table cabinets. Even a washer and dryer was there for him to use. Which he had recently, staying inside only long enough to put in a new load and to bring out the wet things to dry. Two full baskets of folded dry clothing were waiting to be taken in and put away, as a matter of fact. Just getting up the nerve to stay inside long enough to do it was the problem.

He was being stupid, he knew this. But it didn't make him any less afraid of going into his home. Ralph thought seriously about just leaving, giving up his dream of killing a dragon. But he was so broke that if he didn't do something soon, he was going to even lose the house he had now. Things were beyond critical. It was nearly massive destruction phase. Sitting on the chair that he'd set out from the dining room table this morning, he looked at the map he'd been using.

"They're out there. I know it." He had seen them; one he'd even managed to kill, but that too had lost its appeal for him. He no longer wanted to be rich and famous. He wanted.... "What do you want? A warm bed? It's in that thing if you do. You want money? Sure who doesn't, but what will it get you other than more shit?" And now he was talking to himself as well as answering his own questions again. Plus, he was sounding whiney and old fashioned.

He sounded like his mother. She had told him, even as a child, that more did not necessarily mean better. She had lived in the house he grew up in right up until the day she'd passed. The garden in the back of the house was planted every spring and harvested every fall. His mom had even canned things, frozen what she could, and ate from it instead of going to the store and buying things. Which, in his opinion, was so much better.

When he went to let the police in after not hearing from her for several days, he was surprised to find the house exactly like it had been when he was a child. The same couch, same old giant microwave, which he was sure she'd never used, and even the table and chairs that she'd told him once were a wedding gift from his dad's parents.

Newspapers that the Boy Scouts collected were bundled up and tied with butcher's string in the garage. Even her one dish was clean and put away, no draining them overnight for her. She used to say that a washing up needed to be complete. Any fool could leave out a dish to dry all night. It took a clean person to dry them with a towel and put them away when done.

And there his mom had been, in her old night gown, on her side of the full-sized bed. Her comforter was folded neatly at the bottom, her robe lying on the chair near the vanity that held her brush, mirror, and perfume. Ralph had thought it the saddest thing in the world to see that not one thing in his mom's life had moved on after he'd left home. Now he found he wanted to go back to those simpler times.

The sounds in the forest had him tensing up, but he didn't run this time. Instead he watched with his hand on his gun for whatever might come out of the woods for him. And he was sure as he was sitting there that something would. When nothing appeared, he went back to his thoughts. This time he thought of the man who had come by to see him about moving on.

The man, Asher, had told him there were faeries and witches. He was pretty sure that the woman in white had been what she'd told him, and she was now living with Asher and the rest of them. Faerie? He wasn't so sure about them. Not that he thought the man would lie to him, but Ralph wasn't sure. He thought it stupid that he'd believe in dragons but not faeries, but he hadn't really been known for his intelligence.

"Like it matters in the long run." The note fluttered in the small breeze, and he captured it with his fingers. Putting it under his glass, he thought of the vampire and her thug. "See ya...like that's supposed to make me feel better. I don't want you around."

It was daylight now, so that was one of the reasons he'd been spending most of his time out. That and the fact that he really was afraid of getting trapped. The feeling, even in his bed, had him opening windows wide and not shutting any doors in his place when he was in it. Even the cabinet doors had been left open. He felt off his rocker.

"Hello." Ralph held his breath when he heard the small voice. Looking around, trying to gauge if he should shoot or run, he didn't see anything until the voice sounded again. "Down here. I'm on the table."

Lowering his head, he looked at the little man standing on the map. Blinking several times, afraid to move his hands to wipe at his eyes, Ralph let go of his breath when he realized that his head was hurting. The little man sat down, his legs crossed in front of him, while Ralph continued to stare at him.

"I'm Izic." Ralph nodded slowly. "You met me the other week. My mistress and I came upon you in the clearing. She had Bear scare you."

"The woman in white." Izic nodded. "I'm not seeing you, am I? You're my mind going over the edge of Xanadu, and I'm never going to be the same again."

"Xanadu? I'm not sure where that might be. But then I've not traveled much beyond these lands. Where is that Xanadu place?" He said it as if it were three different words. "It matters not. I will not be traveling anymore anyway. I've a job now. Watching over things that are going on. Even the few I have working for me are all but jealous of my new.... I'm to stay focused, she told me. All right then. I have come to ask you to dinner."

"Dinner?" Izic nodded. "Are you going to eat me? Or do you...I don't know, are you going to serve me up to someone?"

Izic stood up and put his tiny little hand on Ralph's cheek. Ralph was so startled by the action that he stayed where he was, even leaned down a little to let him touch him. When Izic seemed satisfied with whatever he was checking, he sat back down.

"You are not feverous or looking ill. I don't know what sort of creature you think might want to eat a human such as yourself, but I don't know that many humans. They are, in my opinion, a quite odd group. Once when we were about town, I saw a man take a lady's handbag. Just ripped it off her arm as if he'd a right to have it. Then one time there was.... Focus, Izic. Focus." Ralph nodded. "Nay, no one is to eat you. You are to eat with us. I was sent to invite you to dinner with the family. It is a celebration of sorts. We have found the king's body, you see."

"King?" Again Izic nodded, smiling this time. "And this king, he's a what? A little person like you are?"

"Oh no, he's the former dragon king." Of course, Ralph thought, dragons needed a king. "And I am not a little person. I'm a brownie. I have...my mistress, she thought you'd be less...I believe she said freaked out if I didn't appear in my real form. Brownies are the most beautiful of creatures if you were to put the question to me. If you don't mind, I can change back now."

"Yeah, okay. Go ahead." The little man stood up but before he did anything...like changing to his true form, whatever that might be...Ralph wanted to make something clear. Lifting his hand up, to show the man he had a question, Izic nodded at him. "I'm already freaked out, just so you know. I have a vampire lover and the man who watches over her watching me, I think. Dragons flying overhead almost all the time that aren't supposed to be real, according to a man by the name of Asher. I'm terrified of my home for reasons I can't really understand myself, and a man, Asher again, came by the other day and told me that he smelled of faeries and witches. Having you as a brownie is beginning to sound sort of normal."

"You are most odd. Has anyone said that to you?" Ralph nodded and watched as Izic shook his body. "There. Much better."

For who, he wanted to ask him. A small...being, he supposed was the best way to describe him, was standing in the middle of his table, with wings. And not just any wings, either. They were sparkly, like someone had dunked the little creature in a bowl of mixed up glitter and it stuck to him everywhere. His face, hands, even his bare feet were bright with it. And then there was his body.

Every inch of it—well, the whole three inches of him—was covered in leather clothing. His boots were a dark brown, his shirt a little lighter than that, and his pants were some color in between. He had no hair on his head, but his arms, which were bare, seemed to have enough for both of their heads. There was a scabbard at his side but Ralph didn't see a weapon, though he figured, since he was looking at a brownie, that he'd just make one appear and cut Ralph's throat out. When he bowed at the waist, then stood up again, Ralph just stared.

"You're not human." The little thing said of course he wasn't. "Okay, yeah, not human. And you have wings. Little bitty wings. You're only about three inches tall and you sparkle like you're one of those disco seventy lights."

"Much larger wings would not be good for one so small, you think? And I am wee, yes, but it's a perfect size for a brownie, don't you think? As for the disco thing you speak of, I've not an idea how to answer that one. I'm no different than most, wouldn't you say?" Ralph nodded, feeling more and more like one of those bobble head dolls that were all the rage a few years back. "You are looking puckish."

"I'm feeling a bit off my feed, yes." Izic asked him if he was going to make it. "Make it? Oh, to the dinner celebration. Okay. Yeah, sure."

He realized that he'd said that several times now, and tried to think what other way he could convey his approval. There wasn't one as far as he could see. Ralph was certainly going to need professional help when he got out of this nightmare. He followed Izic to wherever he was leading him, and Ralph decided that when he returned to his camper, he was heading out. There was nothing worth what he'd been going through in the last several days.

~~~

Ariannona could not believe how much food had been made for this thing. She'd never been to a picnic before and had assumed, like she'd seen in movies or the television, that they'd have a few items in a basket and a cooler for drinks. Then someone would break out a flying disc before they headed to their cars.

"You should really close your mouth." Ariannona did so now with a snap of her teeth. Zak, the dragon to Jed, sat down next to her on the big porch. "You're overwhelmed."

"Yes. Very much so. There are just so many of you." He nodded and tossed a small stone to the gravel drive that led to the garage out back. "Are you sure it's a good idea to have the slayer coming here? What if he decides to harm us all?"

"He won't be able to cross the boundaries of the land's magic if he does." Ariannona knew that but had forgotten. "Besides, sending Izic to get him might wear him out a little. He will have to keep up with him."

"Izic thought it a great honor to have been asked to get the human." Zak said he'd figured that out. "Yes, he can be very vocal when he's happy. I think that is why when I found him he was alone but for his flowers."

The slayer was coming here. And if he even harmed her friend in the smallest of ways, she was going to kill him. But come he was, and for reasons that boggled her mind.

Asher had said he felt badly for what they'd done to the man. First they'd lied to him. Then they'd set upon him with more lies in the form of magic. The man was human, and if they pushed him too far, which Asher thought they had, then there would be no stopping him from bringing other men smarter than the slayer to them, and the dragons would not be safe. Ariannona looked at Zak when he cleared his throat.

"I know there is a difference between faeries and brownies—I mean, other than appearances—but how do they differ in the world as we know it?" Zak flushed slightly. "You'd think someone who has been around for a long time would know that, wouldn't you?"

"Not necessarily. There are many beings that have been here longer than any of us. The mountains know nothing about the sky other than that it warms their backs when they need it and helps the plants on them grow and propagate." Ariannona watched the new dragon hatchlings playing in the dirt by the main house. "It depends on what sort of faerie it is to know what differences there are. Some wake the flowers with dewy kisses. Others put them to bed...you know, close up the blooms for them. Other faeries, they work with the trees and grasses. Some the water. The brownies only have one function as far as I can see, and that's to be with the dragons. And since there are so few of them out in the open, brownies numbers have declined a great deal."

"Sort of like supply and demand that we talked about the other day." She told him something like that. "Izic, he's been with you for a long time then?"

"Yes. Since before I met with your parents." He nodded, and she wondered if he thought about them like she did. Then she remembered that he'd never met them. "Your mother, she was a goddess in beauty. Her hair was the color of her dragon, a deep hue of blue that would darken to black when she needed it to. A protection of sorts when she was skyward in the evenings. Her eyes, the same color as yours, as a matter of fact, were always full of cheer. And when she was pissed, which wasn't that often, they could strike a man down with only a look. Your father was a good man. Funny too."

"Funny? I don't think I ever heard someone say that about him before." He leaned back and so did she. "Caroline said he was fair and stern and helpful. He and my mom would go to homes and help with the sick, and had been known to be in a field when there weren't enough hands around to bring in a crop."

"I saw your mother once, standing by the lake beyond, fishing. I thought it the oddest thing when I knew all she had to do was to shift and eat as much of the fish as she wanted. The lake would have gladly depleted itself for her." Ariannona smiled at the memory. "But just as I was turning to leave her at her silliness, I saw the small child standing by the bushes. I knew that his father had died not long before that. Your mother was trying to talk to him, using what his father had done for their food as a way to break the ice. His father was one of her men, one that had died protecting the queen from a robber while out."

"I wish I had known them. Even for a little while." Ariannona nodded. "I went to the buildings that you showed Asher this morning. I cannot believe how well they have stood up to time. And to think, all this time, they were right there where we could have found them."

144

"The castle would have still been standing today had it not been damaged in the fires. It burned for nearly a month before the smoke stopped curling from it. Some say it was the dragon king laying there, telling them that he lived still, but I knew that he lived no longer. The magic he shared with me, it gave me a connection like none other." She thought of the body they'd found, still preserved almost as if he'd only just died. "Do you know yet what you are going to do with him?"

The crown hadn't been on the king's head, but he'd been near it. The little dragons had not only unearthed the crown for them, but a large part of the dragon beside it. He looked so much like Kiaran that it was as if he was there with them instead of fallen. The dragons who had unearthed him had been bringing all manner of things to the sight, paying homage to their king as if he still lived. Ariannona thought it the saddest sight she'd ever seen, yet beautiful at the same time.

The king's body had been lying on his belly. His dragon form had kept him shielded from whatever elements might have deteriorated him; the scales, they thought, had acted as a barrier between him and the elements. The wings of the beast were close to his body, and when they had unearthed all of him, digging around him so that nothing was disturbed, it was discovered that his body had crushed a man beneath him. Each of them had surmised that it had been the final blow from the man's sword that had felled the great king. No one had said a word for a long while, just looking down at the dead king.

"Asher wants us all to put our thoughts into what we would like to do now that we know where both of them are. He said it was up to us, their children. But Kiaran said that it was up to all of us, because without them, none of us would have been born. I think that Asher was touched by that." Ariannona said that she'd heard he was. "I think I'd like to take him to our mother. Build a tomb for them both to be together after all this time, put it where Mom is now, with the eggs of their children close to them. And a bench too, so that we might go and visit them should we like. I'd also like to use some of the castle stone to make it."

"That's a wonderful idea, Zak. Leaving them in the cave where you were born, it would be fitting for them, don't you think?" He nodded but looked away. Tears were there, even now, for the loss of his parents.

She heard Izic when he spoke, telling her that they were nearly there. She stood up when everyone else did, to welcome the human to their party.

The slayer looked befuddled. An old word, of course, but she could think of nothing more fitting than that. The slayer was coming to dinner. And she wondered what he'd think if he found out that nearly half of the people he was breaking bread with were the very thing he hunted. Asher moved to welcome him.

"I don't think we caught your name the other day." He told them. "All right, Ralph, I'd like for you to meet my family. I wanted you to see who they were so that you'd have no trouble when it came to mistaking them for a dragon."

It was a joke, or was meant to be, but when Ralph took Asher's hand in his, it looked as if Ralph thought it a lifeline and held it tightly in his own two hands. Ariannona watched him, fearful of what he might be about, but she saw the tears then and the fear.

"I don't know what I'm doing." He looked around the semicircle of people and then stared at her. "You said to me, that first day, you were a witch. Asher told me that he smelled of faerie, and I would assume it was you. I'm being terrorized by a vampire too. I can't forget that."

He laughed, sounding maniacal and very stressed. When Asher asked him if he was all right, the man nodded and shook his head at the same time, looking like he wasn't sure what he was. Which she supposed was about right.

"Come on now. Nothing will harm you here unless you get stupid. You're not going to do that, are you?" Ralph said that he wasn't sure he knew anything but how to be stupid. "Don't be so hard on yourself, Ralph. We're going to help you if you want."

"Yes. Yes, I think I want that very much. If you could just get me to the main road, I'll leave you alone. I was dumb for thinking that I could catch me a dragon." He was nodding and no one said a word as he continued. "I'm so broke now that I couldn't afford the gas to get far, and in a few weeks, less I guess, the bank is going to come for my house on wheels. I'm not sleeping well, nor eating either. I'm afraid of my own shadow, and I have.... Why did you invite me here again? I thought it was to have me for dinner, but I know that is probably my mind working overtime again. I'll shut up now."

They had expected to have to talk to him for hours, to try and convince him to leave them alone. There were plans in the works to get him gone. More scares with the "vampire" that Lindsay and Essie had created for him. But he wanted to leave, was willing to do so now, it seemed.

"How much money would it take for you to go?" Ralph asked Elam what he meant. "Just that. What kind of money do you need? To get you going in the right direction. On a better path than you're on right now."

"I don't know." He named a price. "I know that sounds like a lot. It is. But I've sort of been out of work for a while.

You know, pursuing this stupidity. My wife left me. It wasn't her fault, and I think I knew for some time that it just wasn't in the cards for her and me. I just need...I think it's really important that I get out of here. Before the vampire woman comes back and kills me. Or has that guy do it for her."

Ralph was invited to have a seat. When they were all seated, Ariannona asked Izic to have the other creatures of the land stay back. She had no thought that Ralph would harm them now, but the man was close to losing it and she didn't want to push him that far. Ariannona felt sorry for the man.

"I'd like to help you if you'll allow me to. I know this woman friend of mine that is looking for someone to come into her offices and help out. She's an attorney." Ralph nodded, his body perking up a little at the mention of some kind of job. "A couple of times over the last few weeks she's been cornered when she comes from her job. In the parking garage, wherever she goes. This person is trying to get her to give him more than what's ethical. She has a little girl that...well frankly, she's afraid that this man will take her and demand that Jamie do as he wants."

"You mean sex." Elam said that was some of it, but he wanted her to give him Elam's address too. "Oh. She works for you. Okay. You want me to sort of go with her, keep her out of trouble."

"Yes. Do you think you can do that?" Ralph told him that he'd been slightly out of shape of late, but he'd give it a shot. "There will be perks if you take care of her. Her new law firm has a gym you can use. There is an apartment that is up for grabs right now. I can make a few calls and get you something to tide you over until you get paid."

"I have a lot of unpaid bills. I'm not asking you to pay those, but unless this place is free or pretty close to it, I'm not going to be able to afford it." Elam said he'd make a few calls. And when he walked away, Ralph looked at Ariannona. "You're really a witch?"

"I am. Would you like for me to turn you into a frog?" She'd been joking, but he took her at her word and nearly leapt away from her. "I can't do that, Ralph. I was trying to make you laugh."

"Yeah, okay, but don't. I mean, even if you can, please don't. I've had a really stressful few weeks, and I don't think I can take much in the way of jokes. Sorry."

Elbert called them to dinner, and they made their way to the large picnic tables under the big oak.

There were pitchers of tea and water, big bowls of all the food the men had grown up on, and even a few that were favorites of Elbert's. Plates filled when things were passed around, drinks were served, and even a few cookies made their way onto the plates. Ariannona watched poor Ralph as he took what was offered to him but ate little. And when Elam returned, Ralph was told that it was set up and he'd talk to him later.

Chapter 10

Ralph watched the men helping him turn his camper around. He didn't want to hurt any of the trees around him, but he also felt an urgency to leave like he'd never felt before. Now, his head kept telling him; leave right fucking now.

Last night, after leaving the family, he'd made his way to his home. He had a job, money in his pocket to get back to the real life, and a place to stay once he got there. Taking the money out of the thick envelope, he'd laid it out on his table and counted it three times before he stuffed it back in its home. Then he began thinking of the things he could buy with the money.

A better scope for his rifle. A few more shells for his gun. Things that he was running low on…his food, as well as all the other things a hunter like him needed. The longer he sat there, the more things he thought of getting to hunt for the dragons. Because he needed to kill one, he thought. Money like he had now would be nothing compared to what he'd have. Fame and riches were what he wanted most out of life.

Almost as soon as he thought of the dragon he was going to kill, the camper rocked.

"Darling, are you home?"

The vampire. Then the thug shouted that he wanted to come in and suck him off. The woman screamed that she needed to have him fuck her. On and on they went, each of them telling him what they were going to do for him and to him.

They pounded on the doors, the windows. He even thought at one point that they were under his camper, lifting it from the ground with only their hands and feet. Thug had jumped on the roof, caving it in a few times, but luckily it bounced back when he got down off it. Ralph hadn't even gone for his gun, he'd been so afraid that they'd come in and use it on him while he sat there.

Crawling under his table, he put his fingers in his ears so deep he felt the pain of it. But still he heard them, every noise they made, all the things that they did to his camper. His cock hurt, his balls felt like someone had put them in a vise. He wanted to cry. He even did at one point, begging them to go away and to leave him alone.

All night. All through the night they terrorized him. Screaming at him to let them in, begging him to come out and play with them. He knew that they had sex too, right there under the window where he was hiding. Their screams of pleasure only made him sick to his belly, so much that he wanted to puke his guts up and just roll over and die.

And when morning came, their sounds cut off abruptly like someone had turned off a switch and they were silenced. As he stayed where he was, not even venturing out to get a cup of coffee or to go to the bathroom, he knew that as soon as he could, he was leaving there, never to return. Things had gone from scary to really fucked up, and he wanted out.

By the time that Asher and Elam had shown up, he had the camper travel-ready. The sides were in; the canopy was rolled up. He'd even dumped the last of his lake water on the fire pit that he'd not used in several days to make sure that there was nothing to harm where he was. And when Asher asked him if he was all right, he told him what he'd heard this morning.

"They were moaning. The trees were. And I heard the grass...I know you have no reason to believe me, but I swear to you, I heard the grass begging me to leave the place better than I found it, to make sure that I cleaned up every scrap of paper when I got ready to leave." He saw the look pass between the two men and found he really didn't care if they thought him nuts. He knew what he'd heard, and it was the forest telling him it was time to get the fuck out of there. "I'm not telling you a lie. I swear it."

"I believe you."

He didn't, but that was okay. It was his plan not to see any of these men ever again. Not that he had any sort of grudge against them, he just wanted away. Gone forever. And not below the ground as in dead, but away as far as he could go.

When he had the camper turned around, he got out, feeling a little better now that he was on his way. Shaking both the men's hands and then taking the address from Elam where he was going to work for a while, he nodded to them again. He felt there had to be something said, tell them how sorry he'd been about whatever it was he'd shot.

"I guess when I thought about coming here, it was sort of on a lark. I mean in general, not to this place here. I had been chasing these clues, or what I thought were clues, for so long I think I convinced myself that there really were dragons about, and that I was really going to be able to kill one." He laughed a little. "One of them...one that I thought I shot at, he was a big sucker, almost twice the size of my camper when it's all spread out. Now that I think on it, I'm pretty sure that someone would have noticed something that big flying around, don't you? And why on earth did I even imagine that my little guns could bring something like that down? Even thinking that putting iron in the shells was going to make some sort of difference. I was a fool."

Neither man spoke, for which he found himself grateful. If they made fun of him now, he didn't know what he'd do. Getting into the big camper, he waved at them and made his way out the way they'd told him to go. Ralph considered himself lucky that he'd gotten more out of this game than he should have. And he was going to make a good start over too.

~~~

"Mistress? I need a word please?" Elam heard the little man but knew that Ariannona was sleeping, and since he knew for a fact that he and Casdon had worn her out last night, he pulled himself from her arms and went to the door as he fabricated clothing for himself. By the time he was opening the door, he was fully dressed and ready to help out. If Izic was surprised to see him, he didn't say anything.

"What can I help you with? I mean, I can help you, right?" He looked at the stairs and then back at him as he stood on the little table in the hall. "I can go and get her if you'd like to talk to her. But she didn't get much sleep last night, and I'd like to let her rest a little longer."

Elam moved down the hall to the stairs and kept his questions to himself. He really liked the little man. Even respected him a great deal. And he knew that Ariannona depended on him too. As soon as Izic was seated on the table, Elam waited for him to speak.

"Yes. I understand that she needs her rest. Mistress has not been sleeping well since before coming here." Elam said nothing but asked the brownie if he'd like a cookie. "Oh yes, I would love the kind that have the pretty fruits in them. Master Elbert, he has a fine hand at baking."

"He does at that." After getting the cookie out of the jar, he broke it up into smaller pieces and put it on a plate. He thought about getting Izic his own service set, and decided to talk to Gobi the next time he was in town to see about ordering one for him. He also noticed that the man kept pulling at his collar, as if he weren't used to a tie. "What is it that has you up and about so early?"

"My mistress asked me to find some of the other workers to help with the empty buildings that served as the staff work houses. Many have volunteered, sir. It was a great pleasure for them to help with his project. Why, even the littlest ones were—" Elam cleared his throat. One thing he'd learned about the little brownie was that he could get down more streets than there were in a big city to get to the point sometimes. "Yes, the buildings. They're being used, sir."

"Used? I don't know what you mean. Someone lives in them?" He nodded, then shook his head. "You'll have to be more clear on that, Izic. Are there beings living in the buildings or not?"

"The herb room, or drying room as some call it, has an abundance of dried things in it that I think will be a nice addition to the gardens. The bakery, it's going to need some care, but some of it has been started. That's what is living in the building." Elam sipped his tea and tried to decipher what he was saying. "There is a dragon, sir, living in one of the outer buildings, and he is doing some repairs to them. Not all, just the ones with the most damage."

"Have you talked to this dragon?" Izic explained that he was only a lowly brownie and had no way of speaking to dragons. "You're not lowly anything, and I would hope you know how valuable you are to this family."

"Thank you, my lord. You have no idea what that means to me." Elam asked him about the dragon again. "He is old. Nearly as old as myself and the mistress. But he is unwell. Not healthy like the rest of them."

"Them?" Izic nodded and said he was getting to that. "I need for you to get to the *them* part a little sooner please. How many besides the old dragon are living in the outbuildings?"

"Ten. If you count the smaller ones." Elam said that a dragon was a dragon no matter the size. "Yes, I suppose they are. One time when the mistress and I were going along our own way, we came upon a group of dragons that had been tossed from their homes. The smallest ones, we discovered, had such a chip on their shoulders. You would have thought that the mistress or I had kicked them to the curb."

Elam nodded, thinking about the ten dragons living so close. He wondered how they had missed that. Or for that matter, why they'd not come out of the buildings before now.

"How long do you suppose they've been there? I mean, you said little. Do you mean young or just small?"

Izic seemed to think on it and shook his head. "I know not, sir. I do know that there are no young ones, hatchlings as it were. They have been without their mates for a good long time, I think. But I think the bigger of them, the one doing the repairs, he is the oldest of them, as I said." Elam got up and cleaned up the crumbs and put his cup in the sink. "We are going now?"

"Yes. I'm going to contact Casdon and tell him—" He looked at the stairs when Casdon said they were there. "Good. We're going on an adventure. One that I hope will end well."

"End well? Oh my, that sounds like...Izic, what's happened to you?" The brownie said nothing but moved back when Ariannona moved to him. "Yes, there is.... Oh my goodness. You found her? You found her at long last?"

Elam started to ask who, but got it just as Casdon did. Izic had a mate, if the smile on his face was any indication. And Izic was cleaned up and pressed, as Elam's dad called being presentable. The man nearly glowed with his love, and Elam knew just how he felt. After telling him congratulations and telling his brother what they were going to do, the four of them met Asher and Kiaran in the yard.

"You think we'll be enough? There might be trouble. You never know." Elam wanted to point out that Asher was the king of dragons, but Ariannona beat him to it. And she was a good deal less nice about it than he might have been. Maybe.

"You mean the big bad Asher thinks he can't handle this? By all means, go back to bed and let your underlings take care of it." He growled at her and Ariannona laughed.

"They're dragons...I'm pretty sure that they'll be all right. And if not, you can order them to bow before you, and then you can remove their heads. You're a dork."

Elam wasn't so sure about them being all right with this. The dragons could have at any time come from where they were to see them working on the castle. He'd not been down in the other area when they were working, but he thought that they might be able to hear the rocks and such being carried and moved.

As they made their way to the place Izic had told him about, Elam spoke to Casdon, just to be on the safe side.

If something happens, take her away. He said that he would. *No matter what happens to me, you take her away. All right?*

She'll be pissed. Not that I don't like making her pissy for make-up sex, but I don't think this will get her in a good mood. Elam said he didn't care so long as she was safe. *I agree.*

The buildings looked just as they had left them, one of them crumbled and in need of repair or replacement. A great deal of the brush had been cleaned away...the other creatures helping them had done a good job. But in noticing the clean-up job, he noticed the building that Ariannona had pointed out to be the drying room. A lot of repair had been done to it.

Rocks had been moved, and the roof no longer sagged as badly as it had seemed to before. The front door and the shutters along two of the windows had been removed and were in a neat pile, along with some of the things that had more than likely been in the building; a table, some pottery, as well as a couple of things Elam had no idea what they might have been used for.

"Someone has been busy." Elam agreed with Asher. "Look around at the rest, too. Most of the stones are moved from those buildings. And it looks like one of the other buildings has been started on as well."

They moved down the hillside, careful of where they stepped. They could see glass and sharp stones here now that the forest was being cleared out, more than likely falling from the trees from when they'd moved the stones from the castle.

Asher called out to the house and they all waited for someone to call back to them. Elam looked around. It was like he was seeing things for the first time here. He'd been back, once to learn the code to the castle wall and another time just to make sure that he had the code right in his head. But he'd not been here since the clean-up had begun, not on this scale anyway. The buildings, nine in all, were in neat rows, all of them facing the woods beyond. But when he saw a glimmer of something, he tried to think where they were and realized it was a finger of the lake.

"My lord, Anthony?"

Everyone looked at the dragon that came from the building in front of them. He was dressed in armor, his face covered by a heavy hood, and he wore a chest plate, decorated in the crest that they'd found on some of the items in the castle. Golds were tarnished, the silver of it also faded from no one cleaning it, but it wasn't hard to see it was the crest that had been the king's. The dragon came fully out of the building and stared at Kiaran.

"Nay, you cannot be. You were dead. I felt it in my bones like it was happening to myself."

"I'm his son, Kiaran. This is my brother Casdon. This is—"

The dragon looked at Elam and smiled, cutting off Kiaran.

"You are Jacob's son. I'd know that chin anywhere. And the eyes of Sally. I had heard that they were to wed. And here they have a son too." The dragon pulled off his hood and dropped it as he moved toward them. His body was slow to move, Elam noticed. "How? I do not.... I did not know that there were babes of the king and lady queen. And two such fine.... How is it you are here?"

The dragon had been hurt. As soon as he turned to look at him, Elam was taken aback at how bad it was. None of it recent…no, it had happened so long ago that the scars there were faded and dark in places, the wounds long since closed up and healed.

His face had been cut into, deeply. His right eye was gone. In its place was a long scar that had been closed shut by a bad stitch job. And his arm on that side of his body hung limply at his side. There was other damage as well. Some of his scales had burned, and his claws on one hand were chipped badly, worn down in several places. He looked like a war dragon. And Elam remembered them being mentioned at one point during the cleanup.

"You've been working. How long have you been here?" The dragon looked at the buildings, then back at him as if he could not remember exactly how he'd gotten there. He stared for a long moment at Ariannona, but for some reason Elam didn't feel threatened by him. "And your name…I don't think we got your name."

"'Tis you, isn't it? The witch that woke us all." Ariannona said she didn't know what he meant. "We'd been resting. It's what he told us when he took us to the cellar. To rest. I had seen you there, in his rooms with my sister, and I thought that you were to care for the wee ones when they came. But you woke us after he put us to sleep.

Anthony would have...he protected us as best he could, didn't he?"

"I don't understand." Elam shrugged when Asher looked to him for answers. "You're saying that you were a part of the.... Wait, sister? You're brother to the queen?"

"Aye, I am. Her only sibling, as a matter of fact. But I cannot shift as she could. Only a dragon can I be, but that's neither here nor there." The dragon smiled sadly before continuing. "Anthony saved as many as he could that day. We knew there was to be trouble. The household went about its days not knowing that in a few days we'd all be gone. Eve, she told me that I'd be needed later, that Anthony would put us to rest and that we'd be woke someday to be there for the new king." He looked at Asher. "That would be you."

"Yes. I don't know how that came to be, but I've been told that." The dragon looked at Ariannona again as Asher spoke. "You said that she woke you. Are you talking about the day we were here looking at the entrance? That's what the magic did for you and the others? It woke you from the rest that Anthony put you in?"

"Aye. My name is Daniel, brother to the queen by half. My mother, she wasn't a dragon, but my father loved her all the more for it. I was a dragon of war. Not much use after I was injured, but they never took my title away. I think it was because of who I was." Daniel continued to stare at Ariannona. "You've a look of your mother, did you know that? The image is so strong that I thought it her when I saw you."

"My mother? She died when I was but a babe. I was raised by the village." He nodded. "You knew her? You know who she was and what happened to her?"

"Oh, I did. She was a fierce rider, your mother. Rode me through the storms of battle like we were one, she did. Never had a rider before that made me feel like we could win. We did too, win wars that were waged against the dragons. And when she was fat with child, she never gave up her time on my back, taking care of the village and the people in it." When Ariannona staggered, Elam held her. "Then after you were born, we were led to the mountain tops. The army with us was sparse, the war we were waging was only on a few stragglers that thought to take the kingdom's orchards beyond. We won and we were having a great celebration, food and wine that would make our heads ache in the morn. Too soon I guess. We didn't see the party of them coming from the split in the rock. Your mother, she kept us together and fought, though we were both hurt badly. But we won, only by the skin of our teeth, and we went home bloodied. Not a man lost. Or so we thought."

"My mother died, didn't she? That day, that was the man you lost. She died protecting the castle for the king and queen. I don't even know her name. It was never said." Daniel told her and said that he knew not her father. "Zona. My mother's name was Zona."

"Arriving at the castle, like we did, we were taken care of. Each of us were pampered a bit too much, Zona never leaving my side. Had I only looked. Had I just asked her if she was hurt. But my own injuries were great and I thought me to die.... I should have asked her, but I did not." He looked away and wiped at the tears on his weathered cheeks before he looked back at them. "Magic helped me...I lost my eye, part of my teeth. I knew as surely as I lay there that I was done, my heart, my body no longer strong. Zona told me of things she was going to do now, her days of riding into war over. A garden she told me, one that her babe could play by. A cow for fresh milk she'd buy and put in the pasture for me to torment into sour milk. But when I was better, she told me as I lay there, my body starting even then to mend, she told me...made me promise that I'd not be bitter, that I'd make sure that no one knew who you were."

"Why not?" Daniel looked at Asher when he asked. "The king and queen would have taken care of her, right? Raised her as their own?"

"Aye, they might have. But I don't think they knew about her until it was too late. She was lost to them by then, and it took them many years to find her. But they did." Daniel looked at them once again. "She said that men would come for you, being the daughter of a rider. Men did not like a woman who could lead. They liked them less when they carried a man's babe that was not known to them."

"So she let a village raise me so I'd be safe." Daniel nodded. "Thank you for that. I would never have known that had you not come here."

"I've been here. All this time." He looked around and then at Asher. "When the doors were opened by magic, it woke us all. Anthony and Eve, they said that someday the new king would need an army to run the house. A servant to tell them of things past. I knew nothing of what they spoke of. I was old even then and still not at my best. But sleep we did. I know not for sure what happened to them, but felt their deaths as soon as I woke. I knew they were thinking that they were to be killed soon after we were laid down, but as to the how of it, I'm not sure. Nor did I, I'm ashamed to say, know of the babes she'd had. Must have known you'd be hurt too in all that. And now, now we work to restore the mess left behind."

Elam and the others moved around the other buildings and found most of them in very good condition, considering how old they were. Trees had grown up in cracks of the stones on a few. Tables in them were long since rotted and turned back to the earth. The drying room was filled, however, and Daniel told them what each one of the hanging herbs and dried flowers would do. The seeds, he told them, were as good as if they'd been freshly put there.

"Caroline will love this." Daniel asked him how the old witch was doing. "She comes to help us on occasion. Helping with the new magic that we acquire. It's been a trial at times I think, keeping it all straight. She'll be glad to see you."

"She's a good one. Caroline was forever testing her magic on things. Me and the other dragons, we'd let her. We knew that should she have hurt any of us, she'd take care to fix it. But she never did. I will say, I don't know that she knew of this area. Not many did. Anthony thought to keep the castle safe from those that came in under falsehoods." Daniel moved slowly, his body huge but not entirely in good shape. When he stopped abruptly, each of them looked to the sky, thinking they were under attack. He turned to them all with a grin on his badly scarred face. "Have you been inside it? The lower levels?"

"No. We had planned on it. But…. Recently we found the body of the king. And our plans to put the king and queen somewhere was being discussed. I think we sort of forgot about it here." Daniel asked Asher what they were planning to do. "All of us are deciding that together."

"So much like him. You'd think you were his son as well. Anthony would have been proud of you all. Eve too. My goodness, she has babies. Who knew it would come to them so late in their lives?" Asher told him that there were twelve of them. Six sons of Jacob and Sally and six to the king and queen. Daniel nodded, his eyes full of unshed tears. "I've a family again. A great family. Thank you for this. For waking us. When they put us here, hugged us the last time, my heart broke for them. And for me. My sister, my lovely sister, didn't deserve whatever fate had in store for her. And Anthony, he loved his mate with all that he was. I'm sure that they would have loved their boys much the same way. But life, it seems, has plans, and now I'm happy to say that I get to be a part of it again. Come, I've much to show you. And tell you."

He led them to the castle. Elam looked into the dark opening when the stone was moved and said they'd have to come back when they were more prepared. Daniel only laughed and reached inside. With a snap of his fingers the entire place brightened like it was daylight inside.

"Welcome to the castle of the king and queen." Daniel looked at Asher as he continued. "My lord, you must enter first so that the walls know that 'tis you."

"What would happen if someone else were to enter?" Daniel looked at the walls, then back at Asher. "Do I even want to know?"

"The walls of the keep here have been very unforgiving before, my lord. Should one enter now, even after the magic woke us, they would be crushed by the falling stone, their bodies left to rot and show others that this is a kingdom for one and one only." Asher looked inside as Daniel spoke quietly. "You will enter with us and it will see who is there as a friend, and allow them entrance whenever they open the doors. Their hearts, you see, will guide them inward."

"And anyone that enters with them, someone making them come in? What happens to them?" Daniel only had to point to the crushed bones on the floor to the right. "I see. It knows, as you said."

"The magic here, the castle and the land around it, it is far and away the most powerful magic in the world. You will be safe here from now on."

Elam hoped so. It was a scary thought as to how deep they were under the stone above them.

Chapter 11

Asher wasn't sure what he expected when the entire family gathered to enter the lower levels of the keep. Dirt, yes, a great deal of it. Stones that needed to be removed even. But this wasn't at all what he'd thought they'd find down here.

"It's so nice."

He agreed with Essie. It was really nice. The walls stood strong, the path, Daniel told them, had been cleaned when they woke. And the rooms on this side of the long hall, five in all, were as lovely and as pristine as if they might have been only just put together.

"This room is mine. It's a bit bigger than the others. My size and all." Asher looked in when the others did. "As you can see, we had things just so. It mattered little to them that we'd be sleeping through most of the living here. Still do, I suppose. Have it nice, I mean. There was no reason for any of us to believe that we'd be down here so long. But now that I think on it, I guess we should have."

None of the rooms had much in the way of furniture. No dressers to speak of, but then why would a dragon need clothing? There was a smallish room in each of the larger ones, and Daniel explained that they were for personal items they'd brought down with him. He reached into his little room and pulled out the leg guards to his war gear.

"The rest, it was in here too. But when the doors were opened for us, I wasn't sure what we'd find, so I dressed up." He tucked the guards under his useless arm. "I must have been a sight coming out of that building like I did. Glad now that there wasn't a party to greet us. Might have taken me to task and done more damage to my poor old body."

"You did scare us a little." Daniel nodded and moved to the next few rooms. Asher winked at Elam. *I was more in awe of the crest than of him, to be honest.*

Me too. I couldn't believe it when I saw the castle crest on him. They moved on, looking into each room, hearing about the people that lived in them for centuries.

The smaller dragons had been in charge of the scraps in the halls, he told them. They could and did eat what they wanted of it, but for the most part took it to the burn room. Even then the trash had been properly disposed of and not dumped to hurt the land. Asher supposed it was because they were so close to the earth that they'd know long before it was proper to clean up after yourself. There were only but four of them, Daniel told them, but they could work a castle from top to bottom several times a day.

Two of the other dragons, Dane and Wendell, were brother and sister. They bickered a great deal but worked well together. Their jobs had been to guard the entrance. If anyone were to try and come in when the doors were opened, they were to warn the others that there would be a shift in the wall and to hang on. It had been a fun game, Daniel said to him, to see who the castle walls deemed unworthy.

"It only happened once in all the time I was here. Few tried once it was known that coming in to the castle this way, without an invite, would be the end of your life. Wendell, he would ask the names of all that entered, nod once, and then he'd point the way to go. Dane, she'd just watch them, her tail in her hand for whatever reason. I think she thought herself scary. She was, mind you, but the tail thing? I never figured it out to this day. Yes. Only once was all it took." Asher shuddered.

Asher figured that once word got out that the castle was unbreachable, no one would try again. Not with the threat of being crushed to death under stone and magic. When they got to the end of the rooms, Daniel asked them if they were ready for the rest of it.

"The rest of what? I thought this was the only floor." Daniel said that there was one above this one, but he wasn't sure of the condition. "Then I don't understand."

"They knew they were being sieged upon." Asher nodded. "We were very busy up until they brought us down here the final time. Bringing things down to be safe. Not much in the way of foods, mind you, but we did bring down seeds and other things. Eve, she wanted to preserve for you as much as she could."

"What sort of things?" Essie took his hand in hers as she spoke to the dragon. "You mean like paintings and such?"

"Aye, and such." Daniel laughed. "Come. Let me show you what we have for you. I'm sure you're going to.... It took us near a fortnight to put it all here. Working around the others so they'd not have any idea. Then my Eve, she had all the staff leave the castle days before she told us what was to happen. Told them it was a holiday for them, gave them coin to use to have a bit of merriment. I think some of them knew what was going on, had guessed it. But they got most of the staff and others out. Was there a great deal of damage done? I figured fire. Smelled it when I woke, burned my nose at the odor of it."

"The walls were burned so badly that they fell inward. The king, Anthony, he held it for as long as he could. We think now so that his wife could get to safety. I would imagine that they both knew when the other died." Daniel said that they would, their hearts beat as one. "We've been cleaning it out, moving stone to the sides to rebuild. I'm not sure what else we might find, but we have found a book that belonged to someone in the household. It talks about the furniture and who built it. Diagrams of some of the tapestries and art that they had collected. And we've been using it and Elbert's knowledge as to how to get things replaced."

They were moving down the hall again, but took a right at a small split in the stone. Had it not been pointed out to him, Asher was sure that he would have missed it altogether. But as soon as he entered, Asher realized that they had not just preserved things that they could use, but memories for them all.

"As you can see, I think they knew what you'd be about. Eve would linger over some of the things brought here, paintings and such. Somewhere there's a painting of them together too, but I think it in the back of things." Asher nodded as he tried to take it all in. "There wasn't any time to place it well. There was a time when I think we wished we had. At the end, we were stacking things just to get them all in here."

There were paintings of the castle, as well as the woods and mountain behind it. A painting of the lake when it was only just forming. The gardens had been captured in another, while yet another caught the dragons at play. The sky was filled with the images of what Asher was sure were the king and queen, more paintings behind those stacked neatly in long deep rows. Some of them hung on the walls with care, the room's floor too full to hold them.

There were pottery bowls in perfect condition and in as many colors as there were sizes. Baskets that looked like they'd only just been woven. Gourds hung from the beams, their seeds rattling when someone bumped them. There were cups and saucers, tankers and long trenchers. Pewter forks and knives beside spoons to stir with and to serve.

Platters looked like the bits and pieces that they'd seen above when they'd removed the stones. There were bolts of cloth, silk, and cotton in wooden crates that looked as fresh as if they had only just been made, colors still so bright that Asher wanted to take it in the sunlight and see if it was really that blue or purple.

There was a rack of swords, all of them bright with their beauty, the crest at each handle like the one on the chest plate of the dragon who wore it. Chainmail was laid out neatly on a table nearby. Bridles for horses, seats for the dragons who went to war for them beside them. Asher was looking at one of the many books, its pages yellowed a little but the words on the page no harder to read than a newspaper that only just came out today, when Ariannona came to stand near him.

"I have one for you." He turned to look at her. "Dragon book. I took it from Ralph the first time I saw him. I'll get it to you when we return to the house. It's a book of names."

"Names?" She nodded and explained. "He had a book of every dragon ever born and when they died? Who would have given him such a thing? Did they not know that it could destroy all we worked for?"

"Calm your goats. I got it, didn't I? And he got it from Helena. I think he and her were partners of a sort. She would have known his ancestor back then." He asked her where it was. "I have a great many things...not like this, but some that I have hidden away over the years. Not for you. I had no idea you even existed. Nor would I have cared. But I have them."

He wanted to both hug Ariannona and strangle her on a daily basis. She'd burn a person to the quick with her temper and make you laugh at her jokes. Her and her mates, they were perfectly suited, he thought.

"Asher?" He started to tell Elam when he said his name what he thought they could do with some of these things, but then he saw his face. There was something very.... Asher wasn't sure what he could see on his brother's face. He put down the book he had and moved to him, looking too for the source of his concern.

The chest that he was standing in front of was opened so that Asher was behind it. He wasn't sure he wanted to see what was in it. All sorts of things seemed to jump in his head at once. A dead body. The head of several men who had stormed the castle over the years. Slugs or some sort of plague that was going to eat its way into his brain.

You need to stop watching horror flicks. He glanced over at Essie when she spoke to him. *Seriously, all that worry, and all you have to do is walk over and look. For all you know it might be the keys to a new car.... No, it can't be that. No cars then. It could be that it's —*

Okay, you've made your point. He stood beside Elam and looked at the chest. He looked at Essie then. *You might want to come here. This is all about you.*

As she neared them, Elam stepped back but not too far. Asher felt his heart in his chest. The find was going to be...he'd never expected to see this. Not in all of his life. Pulling it from the chest, he held it above her head.

"Essie, my queen, this is for you." She backed up and he laughed. "There's a note with your name on it and everything. The queen wanted you to have it."

"I don't think so." The crown was heavy, and he wanted to see it on her head. "You put that back in there and we'll pretend you didn't see it."

"You can't un-see a crown, Essie. And like I said, she has a note here for you. And it says for the new queen, with your name." She was shaking her head when Kiaran put his hands on her arms. "Come on, love. You have to wear it at least one time."

He'd not noticed until then that the room had grown quiet. Even the rattle of the seeds had gone silent as they all waited to see Essie with the crown upon her head. Taking another step toward her, Elam started reading the note that had been left with it.

"My darling Essie." He paused. "Darling? She must have had you mixed up with someone else. Anyway. My darling Essie. I so wish that I could have seen this upon your head. There is one for Kiaran as well. It is in another case. The three of you, all together on the throne, would have been such a wondrous sight."

"Someone find the case with Kiaran's in it." As they scrambled to find it, Asher looked at Essie again. "She wanted you to have it. Put it here for safekeeping so that you, as a queen, would wear it. Please? For me, put it on one time so that I can see you."

"I don't like you for this." He nodded at her and knew that she really wasn't mad at him. "And a family portrait together is out of the question."

He didn't deny that. Because as surely as he was standing there waiting for her, he knew that she'd sit for one. And it would hang in the front of the castle just like the others had before, he'd bet. When she closed her eyes, he placed the crown upon her head.

The gold of it was as bright as the day it had been forged, with so many diamonds and other gems in it that it looked like a golden showcase just for them, just resting on her head. Dragons adorned either side of the front piece, holding the largest diamond in their hands, their wings spread out behind them. He'd bet that whoever had made this had had the king's drawing in front of him, each detail of it precisely and exactly what he'd wanted.

His, the one that they'd found by the former king, looked just like this one, only this one was smaller and a good deal cleaner. The fall of the stone had only done minor damage, nothing that couldn't be fixed by a trusted jeweler.

Kiaran was crowned as well. He stood behind Essie, the two of them simply too beautiful to use words to describe them. And when he heard a rustle behind him, he turned to see that everyone in the room had gone down on one knee before them. Asher went to his mates and held them in his arms. Christ, he loved these two people so very much.

~~~

Ariannona sat on the hillside and watched the water flow by her. She'd been there for a little while, telling everyone that she'd needed a few minutes. When someone sat beside her, she looked over at Jacob and smiled at him. If it had been anyone else, she might have told them to get lost.

"The weeks before I was summoned to the castle to meet my Sally, I had a chance to see all the wondrous things that his lordship and his lovely mate had been doing for us all. There was little crime in our little world. We had battles and great wars, but there was no theft to speak of. No one went without, and we were happy." He leaned back on his hands and continued. "My mother had passed the winter before, and I'd been trying my best to make a little money so that I might one day find a bride, have a few children, and die at peace with the world as it was."

"Then Helena the black came along and ruined it all." He nodded with a laugh. "Daniel, I remember him a little. He was a good dragon, but I never really had any interaction with him. You and I, can you believe that we were here with that dragon and never knew who he was to Eve? And all that time, he knew my mother."

"I did as well." She turned and looked at him, his voice sounding in awe of her. "I'd not known her as your mother, bless her soul. But she was a sight to behold sitting atop Daniel when they'd be coming or going skyward. And once they were sky bound? Well, I have to tell you, there was nothing I wouldn't have given to have been there with her. She turned heads, she did, walking down the streets, her armor all shiny and dented. Even then, knowing that she was not in my league, I'd think about what it would be like to have her as a bride. But I also knew she'd eat me live."

Ariannona laughed with him. "Daniel told me that she could cut a tree down with a look and a man, too, should he treat her badly."

"That she could. Much like you, I'm happy to say. But she was the kindest person. too, from what I heard back then." Ariannona nodded and looked at the lake again. "You're a lot like her. A beauty in all ways, a look that makes men tremble in their boots. Beauty beyond what a normal man could have ever hoped to touch. And here you are, my daughter-in-law. I'm a lucky man, I am."

"Daniel said she never left his side, not even to get help for herself. He said the one time that she'd started to leave him, he asked her to stay. He told me that he felt responsible for her death for a long time. And for whatever happened to me." Ariannona tossed another rock in the water. "Have you thought about how many lives were touched by them? The king and queen, I mean? How their magic brought us all together, mates for their sons and yours. A castle to put our hearts in. Had they not died that day, do you ever wonder what would have happened to all of us?"

He was quiet for a few moments before he spoke. Ariannona knew that he was a thinker, a great deal like Asher and Kiaran. Jed, she'd come to discover, talked things out, worked the details out for you to help him with, and would write them down, crossing them off as he discarded them. Elam was the same way, a talker and a listener as well. Shane was a man all unto himself. He would sometimes work them out in his head, or just bounce ideas off his head for people to tell him if they would work or not. Gideon, like his brother Asher, would sit for hours working on a problem until he had it worked out to the very last detail. Simeon did neither. He would waste more time doing a job several ways before he'd get it right, neither writing nor talking about his plans until it was done. She liked that most about him.

"I talk to my Sally. Every day I go and sit with her, telling her about my day, something that the boys were up to and what I had thoughts about. She's having me read to her. I do it because she said she likes to hear the sound of my voice." Ariannona started to ask him if he really spoke to her when he continued. "She's stuck there, you see. Something or someone is holding her back. I don't mean to say that she's being held against her will or anything, but she and I believe that there is someone coming that will release her from her grave, and she'll be here as I am."

"The king mentioned you to me. Or at least Sally. He had me repeat a message that I was to give to Casdon several times, making sure that I got it right." Jacob asked her what it was. "They said the love of Sally would bring forth the love of a mother. I told him, but no one seemed to know what it meant."

"I don't either. Sometimes messages can get all jumbled up in your head when you try too hard to remember it. I'm not saying you, but the king, he might have gotten the message all messed up in his head, and that's the reason for you telling him over and over." Ariannona nodded, but she didn't think that was right either. "My Sally, she'd be as happy as a bug in a rug to have these babies coming along. When she passed, it done broke my heart to pieces to have her leave me like she did."

"There's a cradle in the sublevels, did you see it?" He said that there were six of them. All with the boy's names on them with a note. "For their babies. I'm so glad that Daniel showed us what was in there. I knew to open it, but not what we might find inside."

They sat there, neither of them needing to fill the silence. She thought of her mother soaring through the sky with her belly full of her. Of the things that she'd thought had happened to her, why she'd been left alone for most of her life. And she thought of the conversation that she'd had with the lady Eve, too.

"She told me that the magic I got from them would make me different from other witches. I asked her why and she said that they would know that I'd been touched by them." Ariannona thought of the look on her face, and realized even then that she was sending off her future daughter-in-law to meet up with her yet unborn son. "She told me that I could command animals like no one could, that I'd be able to summon them to me when I needed them as well. But she told me most importantly, I'd be forever marked by her. Then she took my arm into her hand."

Instead of telling him what she'd done to her, she lifted her sleeve up and showed Jacob the mark that until recently had never been there. It was a dragon that encircled her entire arm. She told Jacob that Elam and Casdon now had one as well on the same arm.

"She gave you the gift of the dragon." Ariannona nodded and pulled the sleeve back down. "I'd like to answer you now...your question about what would have happened had they not died that night. I think nothing would have changed. Essie would still have come to us. Lindsey too. And you would have wandered into our lives with the message just as they preordained it to happen. The only difference is they would have been here too, to enjoy seeing you all to come together as I have."

"And the rest? The slayer? The man who tried to kill Lindsey? You think they would have been a part of our lives too?" He nodded and said that he knew they'd have to be. "Why? So we'd suffer before finding happiness?"

"Nay, you don't believe that either. I think that they set in motion a great deal of happiness for a lot of people. Yes, they saw to my children and theirs. They provided a good life for me and my family. Much better than it would have been for us should I have simply married my lady Sally." Ariannona asked him about the rest. "You mean the castle and the work being done on that? I think that they would have had something that you would have come together with. Not the castle, but something else equally as large."

"To keep us busy?" He laughed and quoted the busy fingers thing to her. "Yes, being idle has gotten me into a bit of trouble over the years. And most of it was my own fault. I wasn't always this sweet and gentle with folks."

He laughed loudly, just as she knew that he would. Ariannona leaned back so that her back was on the grass and watched the clouds go by her, making shapes out of some of them, thinking idly about the things that she'd seen in her lifetime. The changes that had happened despite the king and queen being murdered.

"I love it here. All this peace and quiet. It's like being here when the castle was new and there was no threat of them dying. The people mostly minded their own business, and when there was an occasional issue, it was dealt with in a timely manner. No one was shot and killed over it. There was no real problem with drugs to make us feel unsafe." She looked over at Jacob. "You did an amazing job in raising your boys. You and Sally, you should be proud of what you've done. It couldn't have been easy raising another man's children as your own."

"It was easier than you might think. We never wanted for anything. There was love there, respect too. Not to say I didn't have to beat a little of the nonsense out of them on occasion, but they were good boys. And have grown to be better men than I could have ever hoped for." She told him he was a good man as well. "Thank you. But you have my

Sally to thank for that. She had a harder task keeping me in line than she did those boys of ours."

Long after he left her, she lay there. It was a very tranquil place and she really was happy to be there. As her eyes got heavier and her body more relaxed, she thought perhaps she'd never been this happy in all of her life.

Chapter 12

Elam reached for Ariannona and was disappointed to come up empty handed. Casdon, he knew, was going to be out of the house for a couple of days. He had some things, he'd told him, that he had to take care of. He knew what a part of it was and couldn't wait for him to come home again. They were having a necklace made for Ariannona as a token of their love, and were to give it to her when he returned. Just as he was going to reach out for Ariannona, to tell her to come back to bed, she moved into his head like a tornado, cursing and pissed.

He is far and away the most...how the hell do you ever have a conversation with him? Asher. He had no idea why, but Asher could piss Ariannona off quicker than anyone. *All I said to him was he should put the books he has in a safer place. I did not tell him to do it. All I did was suggest that having them in his fucking bedroom right out in the open was one of the stupidest stunts he'd pulled to date.*

You told him it was stupid? She said that she had because he was. *And then you wonder why he's mad at you. What else did you tell him?*

I might have mentioned that he's pig-headed and an ass. But that's not my fault either. He asked her why not. *Because he provoked me into it. As I said, he's an idiot, and a pig-headed one at that.*

I see. Elam got out of bed, knowing that she was going to be too pissed off to join him now. *And where is the stupidest man alive that's also an ass?*

You make it sound as if I'm not right in calling him that. Elam pointed out that she might have said it later and not to his face. *And what kind of fun would that be for me?*

He paused as he reached for the shower door. *You wanted to piss him off? Because that's the way I'm hearing it.*

Yes. It's fun. I just don't care so much for when he pisses me off. He stepped under the spray and reached for the shampoo. *He's here, by the way. In our house. He joined Essie and I when we were having a cup of tea with Lindsey. I think he only came here to be a prick.*

Maybe. Or it could have been because I'm supposed to be at the castle with him now and I've overslept. You should have woken me up. She said that she'd wanted so have tea with the women. *They're more important than I?*

On some things, yes. They don't have a lovely cock like you, so you do have that in your favor. He thanked her for that much. *You're most welcome. We've been thinking of a way to have a party for your dad. Did you know that his birthday is coming up?*

Yes, he might have mentioned it. Several hundred times over the last few days, as a matter of fact. He'd also told them that they didn't have to make up for all the ones he'd missed, that he'd be just fine with a small cupcake and a little gift. *Are you going big, and do I have to borrow from the bank to make this work for him?*

I think we have it covered. But you will have to dress up. He asked her why. *We're having a picture made for him. Of all of us. Essie thinks he'd like that. All his sons and their mates in one picture.*

He'll love it. Casdon is picking up his gift from all of us while he's in town too. When we were moving things around a few months ago, we found some old pictures of him and Mom. We took them to be painted on canvas and some color added to them. There was even one of us boys, all twelve of us, sitting on the front stoop of the main house when Simeon was about ten.

Oh, he'll love that. Did the others know? He turned off the water and told her he had no idea, he'd only thought of it when Casdon said he was going by to check on it. *So that's why he left us. I thought...well, never mind. I asked him to pick up a few things for me too. He's going to get me some new shorts and a bathing suit.*

A two-piece one? He felt his cock stretch when she told him yes. *Christ woman, are you going to be wearing it around the house?*

Oh yes, it's all the rage now. Wearing a swim suit in the house while you sweep the floor. He wanted to spank her. *Of course I'm not. I'm going to go swimming in the lake, silly. He's getting you and himself each one as well, but yours will only be the kind men wear, not women who want to show off for their mates. Asher said you guys used to swim in it as boys.*

We did. But I don't think we wore suits. She laughed and he told her he was on his way down. *I'll take Asher out of your hair and you ladies can plan.*

He found Asher still arguing with Ariannona when he entered the kitchen. Neither Essie nor Lindsey were helping the matter either, but egging her on. Asher was losing the battle, whatever it might have been, and Elam thought even he knew that. So after kissing his mate, he left with his brother in tow.

"You saved me back there." Elam told him he could see that. "She's so much fun. I can't tease Essie that way. She cries, and that makes my heart hurt."

"You make her cry?" He told him everything did nowadays. "Oh. Hormones. I guess she hides it well when we're all together."

"Yes, she does cry when she's in bed though. It's all Kiaran and I can do not to join her. And I guess Jed and Zak are having the same issues with Lindsey. Having a baby is really hard work for a woman."

Elam nodded. They'd never talked about children, Casdon and him, and now that they had Ariannona, he supposed it was something that they should bring up. Not that there had been a great deal of time. Things had been a little hectic with the castle and all the things in the lower levels being brought out. And today was a big day for them all.

The stones were all cut, they thought. After going over all the diagrams they had, counting them over and over, they thought they were ready to start laying them in order. The hardest part, as far as Elam could see, had been done yesterday with the women there.

"You think that's what has made her so cranky with you? You know, using up a lot of magic to fill in the floors and walls of the lower levels?" Asher just cocked a brow at him. "Yeah, okay, it's all you. You do seem to bring out the worst in her."

Using as much of the earth as the lady would give them, which Elam was sure still more than she should have, the three women of the family, Caroline, and Gobi had combined their magic and had finished the first of what they hoped were the final steps in getting the castle together. Elbert and his dad had stood by with juice and fruit for them, and when they were finished, falling to the ground when they were too weak to stand, they were fed and pampered until they were better. Mostly when they got irritated with them at the fuss they were making over them.

"We're going to go down slowly, seeing what we need to do on each level as we come up. We won't wander off to explore. There won't be any leaving anyone behind, all right?" Everyone nodded at Asher. He wasn't treating them as children. It was just that like they were, he was a little afraid. The unknown was bad enough, but facing the unknown several hundred feet below ground was something else altogether. "Dad, are you sure you want to do this?"

"Yes." He'd told them all yesterday that he wasn't sure he could be in the castle just yet. Then an hour later, after talking to their mom, he'd come back to say that he was going. No explanation, just that he was going with them. As soon as the light was shone down the long staircase that was leading them to the first of the three levels below ground, Asher let out a long breath and put his foot on the first step. The first of many.

~~~

Casdon moved slowly. He had expected the walls to be cold, the stairs to be slick. They were not just dry, but the walls were as warm as the ground they'd been standing on. But he wasn't taking any chances of falling. Not that he'd be hurt, but he didn't want the rest of them to make him feel stupid. Smiling, he thought of the way he'd gotten back at Elam last night for teasing him.

He'd gotten down on one knee and had taken Ariannona's hand in his. He'd wanted to do this for a few days now, ask her to be their wife. Casdon knew that in the court's and law's eyes she'd be Elam's wife. But in name she was for them both.

"I love you, Ariannona. With all that I am. My dragon worships you. We would both die for you. All of us would." She tried to pull away from him, but he held her fast. "Let me do this. I want this to be right. Okay?"

"Yes. But it's not necessary. I love you both very much too." It was the first time he'd heard her say it. He'd never thought those three little words could instill such a warmth in his body and heart. "You don't have to do this at all."

"No. But I want to. Because we love you as well." She nodded and didn't pull away again. "Okay. I love you. You showed us a way that we would never have found in the castle. You came to us to bring me a message, knowing that you might well die when you gave it. Years and years you waited for the right time, biding your time to do as you'd been asked by our mother and father. For this, my brothers and I would like for you to have this. As a sign that not only do you belong to Elam and I as our mate, but you also belong to all of us as family."

The bracelet was much like the one that Lindsey wore. It was made of dragon's tears as well, but this one had been made with each of his brothers contributing a single sapphire to form it. He clasped it to her wrist and watched her face to see if she liked it.

"This means so much to me." Casdon had said nothing but stood up, keeping her hand in his. Elam took her other hand and they held her while she wept quietly. "I love you all so much. I can't believe how lucky I am that you found me."

"We're the lucky ones. We started this relationship out so badly," Elam told her. "And for that, we will forever be sorry. But Casdon and I have something for you too. From the two of us."

When Elam had nodded at him to give it to her, he tried to hand the package to him. But Elam told him he was much better at romance than he'd ever be. So Casdon had the great privilege of giving their one true love another gift, the gift of the ring that symbolized their love for her.

He was at the bottom of the stairs when Keion brought him from his memories by pecking him on the shoulder.

"It's huge." They were at the bottom of the stairs and looking into a room that was as vast as it was empty. They had known that it would have to be big...there had been a lot of people living and working in the castle back then. Keion grinned as he continued with his observations. "The floor below this one, it's the one to the outer buildings? If so, where is the entrance from there to here?"

"I don't think it's supposed to be easy to find. Essie thought it would be in the southwest corner, so we'll work from there." All of them moved to the walls, and Onimia held the flashlights over them. Casdon was running his fingers gently over the wall when he found a split. "Here it is. I think."

It was indeed the opening to the rooms below. None of them moved to go down this time. The rooms were being emptied by the faeries and brownies, as well as a few dragons. It was hard work, but all of them, even old Daniel, who was supervising the work, said they were honored to do it.

They'd started at the bottom of the newly formed area and were going to work their way up one floor at a time. Zak was in charge of making notes of things they'd need, and Akassa was measuring. So far it seemed that the plans they'd found on the castle and what the women had done were perfect. Casdon moved around the rooms on the next floor up and noticed a light switch on one of the walls. He was staring at it when Elam joined him.

"Is that what I think it is? And have you tried it yet?" He looked at him and said he was afraid to get his hopes up. "Yeah, power wouldn't have been anything that they might have had back then. And when you think of this wall, being solid stone, you have to think there is no fucking way that this will turn on any lights."

"There's an overhead light with a fan too." Both of them were still debating on it when Asher entered the room and asked them if they were lost. "There's a light switch."

Asher, being Asher, went to it, more than likely thinking it a joke, and flipped it on. He fell back on his ass when not only did the light come on, but the fan started going round and round. Elam and Casdon were still laughing when the rest of them joined them in the room.

After that it was a game to find the switches. Bigger rooms had one at each end. The few rooms that had a storage area, like the one they'd seen in Daniel's room, had a light in it too. Hallways were brightly lit. There was even a bathroom, neatly hidden, in each of the five rooms on this floor. They ended up going to the lower level again to see if there were lights there, and discovered a large gathering like room that they'd missed before.

"This is amazing. Do you have any idea how nice this is going to be for the people who work here? Electric and plumbing. I thought we'd be lucky if we got to use these floors for storage, but now we can have people here." Asher was turning the lights off and on as he spoke. Casdon had already decided that should he come here to stay, he wanted the room on the lowest floor; he just liked the feel of being so deep underground.

The rest of the discovery was done much easier. Jacob had staked out the room he wanted, on the first floor nearest to the top. Asher told him he'd hoped that he'd live on the upper floors.

"Nah. I think I'd like it just fine here. Closer to the action of the house."

They all laughed, but it occurred to Casdon why he might feel he *should* have been down where the servants were. Jacob still thought of himself as just a farmer.

"Jacob, I think we'd all be honored if you lived up with the family in the chambers there. You have gone well beyond what was asked of you when my parents asked you to care for us. And having you there with us would make us a whole family again." Jacob hugged him, and Casdon held him tightly. "I love you, Jacob. I truly do."

"Thank you, son. Thank you very much." As he was being hugged by the rest of them, Casdon decided that he was going to make more of an effort to tell him that he loved and appreciated him. The man had literally saved all their lives when he and Sally had taken them in.

They made their way back out of the lower levels, the sun much higher in the sky than they'd thought. As they stood there, waiting for their eyes to adjust, Casdon noticed that it was too quiet.

"Elam?" He said he heard it too. All of them stood in a circle, their backs to each other, and watched, waited for whatever was out there to emerge. Just as he was ready to shift and take to the skies, Asher started to laugh.

"Look. They've been busy." He was pointing to the sky and he could see it now. Daniel and two other dragons — Wendell and Dane — were carrying the largest stones and setting them near the castle walls. Asher continued as one of them, about four feet square, was set on the ground with a hard thump. "We did wonder how we'd get them there without having to carry them between the six of you. I guess bigger is better in this."

In less time than it took for them to look at the lower levels, they were moving the large stones into place. Each one of them had been numbered when they'd been cut away from the mountain. And putting them in place was like working a three dimensional puzzle. One that could crush you if it fell on you.

The work, while hard, was easier with the extra help. He and his brothers, as dragons, were able to move the stones into place while the larger dragons brought them to the area. Daniel had to rest his bruised and battered body often, not as up to the task of bringing in more stone as well as the younger ones, but he was a great deal of help. And by the time they were done for the day, not only did they have a good start on tomorrow's work with the stones there, but they'd gotten up the first six levels of the walls around the bottom.

They made their way to the lake rather than go to their homes smelling like the back end of an ass. The water was warm, warmer than he thought it would be for this time of year, but it felt good. Casdon was in good shape, as good as the rest of them, but that was a great deal of very heavy lifting, and he knew he was going to feel it tomorrow.

Elam was floating on his back when Casdon splashed water in his face. He didn't even rise to the challenge.

"The bathing suit that you got for Ariannona, what does it look like?" Casdon grinned and told him she'd asked him not to tell him. "You've seen it. Why can't I at least have an idea?"

Since Lindsey had joined their family, he and his brothers were able to go into town now. Not the city. The only one that could go there without being on his counterpart's body was Kiaran. It had been wonderful to not only go to the town, but to go alone. He'd had a great time picking up a few things for the house as well.

"She asked me not to tell you. And so you know, I've not seen it on her. Just on the hanger." Casdon smiled as he teased Elam. "Did you know that they can be as skimpy as just a little patch of silk over the nipple? When I was picking one out, I was kind of embarrassed at how little there was to them."

"Oh yeah. How skimpy?" Casdon laughed. "Come on, give me a bone here. I need to know what to expect."

Casdon looked over at the bank of the lake and smiled. "I don't think you have to have a bone, Elam. You can look all you want right now."

"Christ." *Yeah*, Casdon thought, *that about sums it up*. "She's not wearing much, is she? I think...if her nipples got hard, do you suppose that you could see all of her breast?"

"I hope so." He adjusted his cock under the suddenly too hot water. "Why don't we take her downstream, show her how much we love her new suit?"

The plan was great. The doing it, not so much. It took them over forty minutes to get her alone, and then twenty more to get her away from the rest of them. Essie had come with her, as had Lindsey, bringing a large picnic style dinner with drinks and dessert. Casdon was worried that they'd be too late to have any fun tonight when Ariannona stood up and simply dove into the water.

It was a sight to be marveled at, her sliding into the water like a water nymph. When she came up for air, only to go back under and swim upstream, he watched her like a starved man. It wasn't until Essie laughed that he tore his eyes from her.

"You going to sit here all night and let her wear herself out by waiting for the two of you, or are you going to go after her? Christ man, do you need instructions?" Casdon said no and looked at Elam. "Go. Before I have to tell her that you two would prefer to sit here and stuff your faces."

Casdon took off to the water and dove in. He wasn't as good at it as she'd been. He hit the water more like a rock than a swan. As he made his way in the direction she'd gone, he thought of all the things he wanted to do to her, and nearly swallowed the lake when Elam shoved his head under the water.

"The first one there gets to eat her first."

Casdon took the challenge and doubled his efforts. Then he smiled and let his dragon take him and took to the skies. He'd be there a long time, feasting on her, before Elam got there. As soon as he spotted her, lying naked on the bank, Casdon landed softly beside her and took his body back.

"Elam said you'd pay for that." Casdon said he didn't care. "I don't either. Come here. I need to touch you."

Not to deny her anything, he went down on his knees between her outstretched legs. "I'm going to enjoy this. And you."

He was just pulling her pussy to his mouth when Elam came out of the water. Yes, he'd cheated, but he really didn't care. Not with her spread out before him.

Chapter 13

Elam took her mouth and did the most amazing things to it. His hands touched her breast, her neck, even her throat in ways that made her want more. Need more. Casdon was at her pussy, fucking her with his fingers and tongue. Her body burned for them, ached too. Even as she was coming, bowing up off the ground, they were moving her, adjusting her to take her again and again.

"Come for me, love. I wish to taste all that is you." Elam had switched places with Casdon. His tongue was thicker, quicker than Casdon's, but no less talented. The cock at her mouth made her hungry.

Holding his balls as he fucked her mouth, she watched Casdon's face, saw how much he enjoyed what she was doing to him. And when he jerked his cock from her mouth, fisting his cock, she cried out when his cum sprayed over her face and breasts.

Elam moved up her then, biting her, then kissing the tiny wound. He took her breast in his mouth, suckling it until she begged him to take her, Casdon doing the same to the other. And then she felt the cock, Elam's thick cock, at her pussy. She cried out when he took her hard enough to take her breath away.

Casdon watched them, stroking his cock up and down as Elam fucked her. With each stroke of his cock, touching the sweetest spot in her body every time, Casdon's hand would be in time, his balls tight against his body.

Loved. She felt so loved that she had to squeeze her eyes shut trying to hold in all the emotion. And when Elam said her name, she looked at him and saw his love reflecting back at her.

"Fill me, Elam. I need you." He cried out, his body bent back as he came, saying her name over and over as he emptied himself in her. When Casdon came, his cock once again at her mouth, she tasted him, his juices sliding down her throat as she released as well.

Almost as soon as Elam dropped on her, he was moving to the side. Casdon helped her turn to her belly, lifting her ass up as his cock took the place of Elam's. He pounded her, his hand digging deep into her hips, his hips slamming against her so quickly that she felt his balls when they touched her pussy.

Telling Elam to come to her, he moved to be under her head, his cock at her mouth. Taking him deep, using the momentum that Casdon was creating so she could fuck him, she swallowed him down past the tightness of her throat and was rewarded with his body jerking to another powerful climax.

"Again. Come again." Casdon bit down on her shoulder when he spoke to her, his voice tight with his need, his body hard with his desire. When he bit her, tearing into her shoulder, she came again, bringing Elam with her when she cried out around his cock. Ariannona had too much, her body spent. She simply fell where she was.

When she woke she was home, in their bed, both of them on either side of her, holding her between their warm bodies. She felt Casdon nibble at her shoulder, but he didn't stir. Elam pulled her hand to his mouth and kissed her when she looked at him.

"I love you." Ariannona told him she loved him as well. "When the castle is finished, I want us to take a trip, the three of us. I've talked to Caroline and she's going to see if we can go somewhere that Casdon can be a part of us."

"I'd like that. Very much so." He nodded and held her. "What else? You're holding something back. What is it?"

"Ralph called me today. He wanted to thank me for the job, as well as the money to get a new start with." She nodded. "He met up with Jamie, and it turns out they're dating. He's about as happy as he could be right now. But he wanted me to tell you something."

Ariannona held her breath. She'd told them all about what she knew of Ralph's family. And that they had been responsible for killing more than a couple of the older dragons in her time. Whatever this man wanted, it wasn't going to be good.

"Tell me." He nodded but still didn't speak. She knew it was going to be bad when he kissed her hand again. "Please, just tell me."

"There are two more men coming. Not for the dragons. He said that they're after you, that one of them had it on good authority that you're what he knows you to be. A witch." She nodded, her heart in her throat. She'd been hunted before, being a witch. Back when they burned her kind at the stake. "We'll protect you from them. I swear to you, none of them will get close to you."

"I believe you." He held her and she felt Casdon stir and hold her tightly. "We have to let the others know. Caroline and Gobi. Any of the witches in the area, they'll have to be warned too."

"Are there a lot?" She told him about five. "All right, we'll gather them together and let them know what—"

"No. Not together. Most of them don't know who the others are. Witches aren't a.... We're not a social bunch. We'll tell them, the ones that I know, and the others will find out when they see Gobi. Most of them go into her shop when they need something."

"Yes. All right. You would know best." She nodded and lay there, thinking of the last witch she'd known to be captured by a zealous group. She asked Elam if it was just a bunch of men or an order. "They call themselves the Herald. I'm not sure why, nor did Ralph know. But he said that he'd let us know everything he did. He has some really strange friends."

"I'm sure he does. The others, do they know?" Elam told her that he'd planned on telling them tonight, but got distracted. Ariannona smiled in the dark. "You liked it, I think."

"I did. Very much so."

She lay there long after he fell asleep and thought about the men, the Herald coming for her. She'd dealt with them, not in many years, but she knew that they were a group that thought anything that wasn't them—human—was the work of the devil and that they had to be destroyed. She reached for Caroline to let her know.

I thank you. I'll be coming to the land tomorrow. That should keep us safe. Would you ask if it would be all right if I brought Gobi too? She's not safe alone anymore if those idiots are back.

Didn't you have a round with them a few years ago? She told her she had. *I think I heard that you killed one of them.*

Three. But they were hurting one of our kind. Do you suppose that they've figured out where I am, or that it's only a lucky guess? Ralph told Elam they were after me. I don't know how they found me after all this time. I've not left the area. Caroline said she'd look into it. *Thank you. And when you come here, don't forget to bring your books. We might have a need for them. I have...I'll have to go and get my things too. And Gobi, if she still has hers.*

A witch is never without her things, my dear. You know that. She did. But it didn't make her feel any less afraid of these men than it did before. *We'll also set up that garden that Asher was talking about. The herbs he said that they found in that building might hold the ticket to a great many spells that have long since been put to rest.*

That scares me as well. What someone might do with the things in that drying room. I've put some faeries on it, watching it. But you never know what might come. Caroline said that was true. *All right then. I'll see you soon.*

Ariannona wasn't afraid for herself, but for the dragons. If the people coming for her even got a hint of what else was here—an earth faerie as well as the dragons—there would be no stopping the onslaught of the monsters coming for a piece of any of them.

~~~

Erin wasn't sure what she was supposed to do now but die. There wasn't any way that she was going to live through this and she knew it. Running along the streets, trying her best to stay at least one step ahead of the monsters behind her, she tried to think. Not normally her best thing to do even under the worst kind of conditions.

"Well, this is about as bad as it can get, Erin girl." Talking to herself made her laugh. "Too late now to change what I do."

The shot behind her tore a hole in the frame of the door she was standing in front of. Taking off again, holding her belly, Erin dodged empty stalls in the market place as well as ones full of merchandise. One man tried to stop her, more than likely to help, but she was beyond that now. *Run*, her mind screamed at her.

She needed to vent her wares. Erin had no idea what it was really called—giving away one's magic was something that she'd known about her entire short, terrible life—but she knew that if she could find someone to take it, her magic, they might be able to help the next person these men came after. She looked down at the bloodied wound in her belly and felt the pain of it all the more. Reaching out, she felt for the strongest person she could find and found three.

I'm dying. The man, whoever he was, told her he'd help her. Erin felt the sting of tears. It had been forever since anyone had said those words to her. *There's no time. I need to vent to you.*

Vent? I don't know what...what are you? She told him. *A wolf. I'm a dragon. My name is Kiaran. Tell me where you are and we'll come for you.*

You'll never make it. They're coming now. I've been shot with silver. I'm as good as dead. He told her that he could be there soon. His dragon would bring her to safety. *I need you to accept all that I—*

The pain in her leg took her to the ground. She tried crawling then, anything to get away. But the man, whoever it was, put his booted foot on her back and she lay down. Kiaran was screaming at her in her mind to tell him where she was just as she was flipped to her back.

I'm dying. He said he was coming. *Will you accept all that I am? Will you take what I have to offer, use it to find these bastards?* The gun was put to her forehead. She begged the man in her head for an answer.

Yes. I accept. It left her, everything she was. All that she might have been. Even her memories, from birth to adult, left her. But more importantly, so did the memory of the face of the man in front of her. *I'll find him. I'll end him.*

She watched as the trigger moved back, the man's finger tightening against the guard that held it. Thanking Kiaran, she closed her eyes. It was done.

Now Available in the Dragon's Savior Series

Asher
Dragon's Savior
Book 1

Jedidiah
Dragon's Savior
Book 2

Elam
Dragon's Savior
Book 3

Before You Go...

HELP AN AUTHOR

write a review

THANK YOU!

Share your voice and help guide other readers to these wonderful books. Even if it's only a line or two your reviews help readers discover the author's books so they can continue creating stories that you'll love. Login to your favorite retailer and leave a review. Thank you.

Kathi Barton, winner of the Pinnacle Book Achievement award as well as a best-selling author on Amazon and All Romance books, lives in Nashport, Ohio with her husband Paul. When not creating new worlds and romance, Kathi and her husband enjoy camping and going to auctions. She can also be seen at county fairs with her husband who is an artist and potter.

Her muse, a cross between Jimmy Stewart and Hugh Jackman, brings her stories to life for her readers in a way that has them coming back time and again for more. Her favorite genre is paranormal romance with a great deal of spice. You can visit Kathi on line and drop her an email if you'd like. She loves hearing from her fans. aaronskiss@gmail.com.

Follow Kathi on her blog:
http://kathisbartonauthor.blogspot.com/